LITTLE BIRD

TIFFANY MEURET

ISBN (print) 978-1-64548-061-7
ISBN (ebook) 978-1-64548-062-4

Cover Design and Interior Formatting
by Qamber Designs and Media

Published by Black Spot Books,
An imprint of Vesuvian Media Group

This is a work of fiction. All characters and events portrayed in this novel are fictitious and are products of the author's imagination and any resemblance to actual events, or locales or persons, living or dead are entirely coincidental.

To the grief-stricken and sad. Skelly was my lifeline when I wrote this book. May her infuriating and constant presence be a comfort to you as she was to me.

Other Books by Tiffany Meuret

A Flood of Posies

DAY ONE

THE MORNING WAS always too bright after a bender. Well, perhaps not a bender, but a carefully controlled evening of adult beverages that had gone slightly off the rails. She'd allotted herself two drinks in which to imbibe, but after her second pour noticed she only had enough vodka left for half a drink and figured why not kill the bottle? The additional serving had been more than the half drink she'd anticipated. That was a packaging issue and she refused to be held accountable for their manufactured deception.

Sunglasses pinching the bridge of her nose to protect herself from a light-induced migraine, she went to sip at her coffee and remembered she'd yet to make any.

Po, her chihuahua, yapped at her from his usual spot in front of his empty food bowl.

"Coming," she said, though this did little to soothe him. It wasn't until the food cascaded into his plastic bowl that he quieted long enough to scarf down his breakfast, acting as if he hadn't eaten in days. His last meal hadn't even been a full twelve hours earlier, to which the vet would complain about his ever-growing weight again, but the vet wasn't the one living with the mouthy beast. Life was too short to deny the little guy the simplest of pleasures, things like a good meal and a long nap, both of which he'd mastered in his two years of existence.

Monday arrived whether she approved or not, and though she worked from home she still needed to maintain some semblance of structure. She fiddled with her failing espresso machine, a wedding present regifted to her in the divorce settlement. The thing didn't always turn on and sometimes needed to be unplugged and plugged in again before it'd power up, but she had a way with her patched-up appliances—a few good curses and a whack to its side always woke it up. She packed a double shot and waited for the water to heat.

Po, long finished with his kibble, leaped onto the plush pillowtop chair she kept near the kitchen table for him. Her coffee hadn't even dropped before he began to snore.

Only eight in the morning and she was already dreaming of bedtime, but here she was, same as every day–Monday through Friday, eight to six, all federal holidays excluded. Her laptop whined as the fan kicked on, circuits daring to spark under the constant strain of use. The coffee tasted sour, but she chugged it down in a gulp before checking her email.

She called her service Premium Client Unlimited, a name so intentionally vague that nobody could hold her to any sort of standard, as no one could even describe what it was that she did. If pressed, she usually referred to herself as the silver-tongued spinster. Realistically, she was a glorified carrier pigeon, a messenger, emailing the clients of her clients to resolve disputes when business owners, independents, and freelance workers had run out of ideas. Sometimes she collected payments, sometimes aided as an intermediary when communications crumbled. The gold plan was $99—which was the package that most people still willing to entertain her nonsense usually chose.

For that price, her customers would receive one fifteen-minute phone call, three email translations, and her handy guide to navigating the modern customer, which was largely populated with spiraling analogies of her own creation, and a pocket guide to responding to angry complaints in the digital realm. She banked on the fact that nobody bothered to read it, but on the rare occasion someone asked her to extrapolate on her parable of pepper in the fan, she would respond with, "Think back. You've actually already answered the question yourself."

To this day, no one had contested this assertion. Well, no one besides her ex-husband, Stuart, who managed to challenge everything and anything about her as if he was looking to impress a corporate sponsor in the sport of it. But she wasn't thinking about Stuart today. The divorce meant she was done thinking about Stuart. Period.

This was where the magic happened, where her clients emailed her their customer service woes, often in expletive-filled rants, that she, in turn, translated into professional soundbites to encourage positive discourse between her clients and her clients' clients. This, of course, was impossible, as clients were terrible creatures with discounts-for-brains and herbivore teeth that weren't terribly sharp, but so persistent and dull that the thought of hearing them chew up another complaint made one want to scream until their voice box radiated itself to death. Naturally, her clients were no exception, but they paid her bills—most of the time.

Her Monday inbox was an impressive sight—swollen under the load of business-casual bickering and hurt feelings. A normal Monday populated about two-hundred-and-fifty orders, most of which were simple one-off conversations that she could spin in her sleep. Completing these would take her into lunch, and she'd spend the rest of her day responding in varying degrees to follow-up emails and new orders.

Today was slightly more boisterous than the norm, a cool three-hundred-and-sixteen orders already populated. Sometimes, she marveled at her success at filling a niche in the industry that nobody knew they needed. In all actuality, they did not need it, but they didn't know that. Some days she reveled in her good fortune. She, a bonified, platinum business bitch, spewing arrogant slogans like: "A fool and his money are easily parted," but that never lasted. Most of the time, the concept of her business just made her sad. She'd feel guilty, like a vampiric con-woman looking for the next mark. Then, one of her clients would email her something utterly obscene and she'd forget all about her previous reservations and ensuing existential crisis.

Until the next day, but that was for her to worry about later. For the moment, she was flush in the center of a confidence boost, proud of the small uptick in business.

The hours whizzed by with the furious clicking of her typing. One of her more consistent clients, Jackie, was at it again, and once he got rolling, he was a tough boulder to stop. One of Jackie's customers was disputing an invoice and threatening to call the cops on him for theft. This was a bluff, but it was bluff enough to send Jackie into a fury spiral so monumental he mentioned to Josie he had a few buff cousins up north that would be thrilled to assist him. This, too, was a bluff, and it was Josie's job to translate his attempted assault into a professionally appropriate message.

Although, committed to memory, she checked her pocket guide for a proper translation. Sometimes physically looking at it helped clarify her instincts.

PREMIUM CLIENT UNLIMITED
HANDY TRANSLATION GUIDE

- I see your point= And it's stupid
- I understand why you feel that way= And it's stupid
- I just wanted to check in= to see what stupid shit you are going to make me deal with today
- Is there anything I can help you with= I'd rather eat my arm off the bone than help you
- Would you like to schedule a meeting to discuss further= I would like to tell you how wrong you are again, but this time to your face

- Can you please clarify= Explain your nonsense
- I do not like to leave an unhappy client= Not because I like you but because you'll trash me all over Yelp
- I apologize for the inconvenience= The inconvenience to me for having to deal with you
- What would you propose= I hate your presence in my life and will give you whatever you want to ensure that I never have to speak to you again
- Cordially= fuck you
- Warm regards= fuck you
- Hello= fuck you
- How are you= fuck you
- As per our last email= Can you read? Also, fuck you

It was a working list, scribbled and scratched and written in the margins of a formerly white scrap of paper taped to her laptop. The responses were instinct now, and she'd provided a less offensive outline of them in a PDF to all her gold-level clients. On occasion, she would lose business to the proactive few who utilized it, but those were usually the most satisfied of any of her clients, and the ones she pursued for testimonials and reviews, of which most happily obliged. Therefore, bringing in more new clients and replenishing her well.

Then there were the Jackies. He was the type to keep her on retainer as if she were a posh New York lawyer. His business is what would eventually replace her espresso machine.

Jackie,

I understand your feelings here, and I, too, would be very frustrated. Yet, instead of upsetting the situation further, I suggest letting your client lead this conversation. This will promote a sense of being heard and foster satisfaction, which in turn, fosters money into your bank account. As you admit, this is the only reason you show up to this business day in and day out, through all the bullshit. Please see my attached recommended response. Please follow up with any questions or concerns!

She attached her most popular form letter—resolving financial disputes was her most prolific service—knowing full well Jackie would ignore all of it. He had a knack for upsetting his customers beyond recognition and then paying her hundreds of dollars to avoid a lawsuit costing thousands. She liked Jackie, yet couldn't stand him. She supposed she felt that way about most people.

Conveniently, as if sensing the wayward thoughts of her daughter from her San Diego marina, her mother texted her.

I saw a seal today

> Was it a seal or a sea lion?

Probably a sea lion I guess why

> Curious

It was spitting water around like a whale

> A whale?

You know like a whale with their blowhole it was cool

> Neat
> Did you get the toilet fixed?

NO but I use the marina bathroom. Arv said he would fix it next time he was up

> Who's Arv?

My neighbor

> Oh

You should come visit me

> Maybe in the spring

So a few months

Easter break

okay

k

Josie set her phone face down on the table, hoping to discourage any further conversation. The phone buzzed several more times, but she ignored it.

Po squirmed in his seat, well attuned to her shifting moods, which signaled the time for a treat and a cup of tea. Her morning dose of ibuprofen was no longer containing the foggy lull following the previous night's bender. She tossed a milk bone to Po, who didn't deign to remove himself from the chair, then prepped her electric kettle and a fresh set of pills. This would get her through the second half of the day with as little ass-dragging as possible.

An entire row of her pantry was dedicated to tea, both bagged for convenience and loose. Green tea was her favorite, followed closely by almost any other form of tea, with black tea making the list only due to obligation. She drank it rarely, usually only when her sinuses were jammed up and she couldn't taste it very well.

As she gazed out the window overlooking her brown yard, she spotted something odd. For years nothing had grown in the neglected dirt lot Josie called a backyard, and she had no idea why anything had sprouted now. A green bud surfaced dead center in the brown expanse, standing out like a marble in a riverbed. Probably a weed. It'd been a wetter winter than her desert town was used to, but even then, this weed must possess fortitude far beyond her negligence. She wondered what kind of plant would spontaneously bloom in such a way.

This weed must be a renegade, which was respectable.

Ibuprofen digested, she chose an oolong tea as the end cap to her short work break. She was about to resume the daily grind when the measured beeping of a reversing truck interrupted her rhythm. It was close, very close. Like, in her front yard close. She did not appreciate this at all.

Over the few years she'd spent in this cul-de-sac, she'd grown quite attuned to its daily schedule. The house to the west kept a timely, evening routine. A small car left every evening around seven p.m. and arrived back around seven a.m. The one next to that housed iguanas and an old married couple who largely kept to themselves aside from major holidays. The two houses directly across from her were infested with children that sprinted banshee-like through the streets every evening and weekend, but all were school-aged and blessedly absent during working hours.

Then, there was the house to the east of her—a ramshackle thing overrun with untreated termites and oil stains, serially rented out to the lowest bidder, none of whom ever lasted more than six months. The landlord made infrequent appearances when it was unoccupied to prune weeds in the hopes of attracting another sucker to sign his likely illegal rental agreement. Josie had witnessed many a type wander through those walls—some with families and kids, some with coolers and midterms, and some with nothing but folding tables and a few boxes. The place was a black hole—sucking at the tit of decency until it was nothing but a used husk of its former self. It'd seen some shit, that house, and it'd stolen a bit from every person that had ever dared to leave it.

Without having to look, she knew it had found another soul to claim. The beeping stopped, and the rumbling engine of the moving truck cut away. Tea in hand, Josie pulled her front curtains back a finger's length to snoop.

The moving truck was on the smaller side, not big enough for a large family with equally large amounts of crap to move. One, two people tops. She waited for someone to reveal themselves so she might get an idea of what kind of neighbor she'd have for the next few months. College kids were loud little assholes that didn't care about the weeds or the termites or much else either. Single men were depressingly silent, yet tolerable because of it. Single women, however, especially older white women, were the ones Josie detested the most. They were chatty and lonely and demanded attention at every possible opportunity. These were the neighbors Josie observed through her peephole, waiting for them to disappear into their home long enough for her to escape to her car. These were the type to demand camaraderie in their singleness, to demand friendship, reciprocity optional.

When her new neighbor finally walked into view, Josie cursed to herself before taking a long, bitter sip of tea. "Of fucking course."

A salty-haired woman, perhaps sixty plus years old, appeared at the rear of the truck attempting to coax the back latch open. She wore a purple fanny pack and a beige camping hat with a feather dangling from one side. Josie pulled back from the curtains, afraid the woman might catch her spying and want to chat, but the woman was more enthralled with the latch of the truck than entertaining neighbors. After pulling on it for a minute with no success, the woman kicked the latch with her steel toe boots and it popped free.

Josie let the curtain fall and went back to work.

The woman emptied her truck in a matter of two hours. Josie knew this because she had been watching her through the curtains the entire time—in between emails, on her way to and from the bathroom, just to stretch her legs, or because of a loud thud that made Josie wonder if the woman had gotten herself crushed under a refrigerator.

Po was also distressed, sprinting toward the window at every scratch, sniff, bang, or creak, hairs standing in a line down his spine as his snout pulled the curtain up from the back of the couch. He constantly yapped as if perpetually forgetting this woman existed despite having barked at her all afternoon. The new neighbor had probably already figured out Po's name just by the sheer amount of times Josie had shouted at him to knock it off, a command he adamantly refused to obey.

By six in the evening, the moving truck had sputtered away, and Josie relished the thought of some peace and quiet. Queuing up her favorite post-work playlist, she fixed herself a vodka soda and ate a granola bar before diving into a bag of stale tortilla chips.

By the time dinner was eaten, she'd already refreshed her drink twice. Her third vodka soda—a little less soda in every iteration—left sweat rings on the arm rest of her suede couch, long since destroyed by both the dog and her drinking. She hadn't bothered to keep Po off the couch in a year, not after she puked all over one of the cushions and stained it strawberry daiquiri pink.

"Sensible," she said to Po simply because he was the only other one there. "Tonight, I need to be sensible. No hangovers. Right, Po?"

Not that it mattered much. None of her Tuesday customers would know she was hungover. In fact, she often performed her best work when a little wrung out. Still, it was never wise to start a week off in the same fashion she ended the weekend.

The television blathering in the background, she decided to toss her third drink in the sink and call it a sensible evening when headlights darted across her window. The new neighbor, probably coming home after returning the moving truck. They flickered again, and a third time shortly after that as if the woman was circling the cul-de-sac.

Po launched himself at the windowsill again, seemingly

appalled by the interruption. Josie clutched her glass and pulled the curtain back to see what the hell was going on.

"What … the fuck is this?"

Sipping her drink, Josie watched her neighbor circle the cul-de-sac two more times before finally stopping.

In front of Josie's house.

The wrong house.

Jesus Christ Almighty, this woman was a trip.

Her little Subaru still humming, she poked her head out of the car window and cursed, then backed out. One last, crawling loop later and she'd finally gotten it right, successfully parking in the correct driveway and disappearing into the house.

By the time Po had finally collected himself, Josie had unthinkingly finished her drink and was running a nervous finger over the rim of her empty glass. She had a bad feeling about this woman, something guttural and instinctual was telling her that this lady was an invader. Before she'd even rinsed her glass and loaded the dishwasher, Josie envisioned five different ways in which she and this new woman would clash, from mailbox hostage situations to inviting herself over for cookies to regaling Josie about every bowel movement her grandson in Tallahassee ever made. Josie cringed so hard she might have sucked her teeth down her throat.

This was going to be a nightmare.

Which was certainly true, but not for any of the reasons she expected.

DAY TWO

THE WOMAN WAS standing in Josie's front yard, staring at something. Nothing.

Josie awoke in a surprisingly good mood that morning, attributed entirely to the fact that she'd forgotten all about her weird neighbor. Once she remembered, her first instinct was to peek through the curtains to get a gauge on this new person's morning routine. This woman had already managed to make an impression on Josie just by unloading her moving truck, so she was expecting *something* slightly off—grabbing her paper from the yard in her underwear or summoning up an army of lawn gnomes the neighborhood kids would steal or powerwalking the cul-de-sac at ungodly early hours. What she did not expect was to look through her front window directly into the back of the woman's windbreaker.

Minutes passed before either of them moved—the woman staring at whatever held her attention, and Josie staring at the woman. Thankfully, Po had bypassed this debacle entirely and waited impatiently by his food bowl, otherwise, he would have lost his mind and given away Josie's position. Finally, having deduced whatever it was she came to deduce, the woman nodded knowingly and tromped back to her property, careful to walk lightly on the gravel.

Whatever reservations Josie initially felt now quadrupled. This lady was a shitshow. Josie already counted the days until she might move away. Six months, tops. That's all anyone ever lasted, and then this woman, whoever she was, would be nothing more than a curious memory.

Po barked from the kitchen, increasingly impatient as the seconds passed.

"It's not right," she said as she filled his bowl. "Standing in another person's yard like that. She doesn't even know me."

She beat at her espresso machine. "What if I was crazy? She wouldn't know if I had a gun or whatever."

The espresso machine obeyed. "She practically tiptoed back to her house, so she knew how inappropriate it was. She didn't want me to know."

Ceramic clinked together as she searched for her favorite mug in the dishwasher. "So, what was she doing there? And why did she pull into my driveway last night?"

A double shot of medium roast coffee leaked into her waiting mug. "Oh, I got it!"

To this Po allowed a small pause to his eating and glanced up at her.

"She's fucking batshit."

Josie patted Po on the top of his lemon-sized head. He growled possessively in return. Someone obviously had his tiny panties in a twist, but she let it slide. Something in the air today was bringing out all the oddballs. One glance at her laptop made her chest tighten—who the hell knew what awaited her in there. Maybe Jackie got into a fist fight with that customer of his. Or maybe she was getting threatened with her own lawsuits. Or maybe she had some new bad reviews. Who knew? That was the rollercoaster ride of customer service—thrilling for one second and then you throw up.

The weed that had captured much of her attention the previous day had all but evaporated from her thoughts. That was until she glanced through the window and saw what it had accomplished since the last time she looked at it. The thing had exploded. Green tendrils laced from the epicenter in an intricate web nearly ten feet in diameter. The tiny bud of yesterday was now a foot-high shoot, aggressively reaching toward the sun. Josie stood dumbfounded in her kitchen trying to process it all. This was beyond her—she explicitly avoided all gardening due to her inability to keep anything alive, well except for Po, but that was more a success on his part than hers. Otherwise, she'd been miserable at keeping even the simplest flower alive for longer a day. Her ex used to bring her flowers until he found a vase full of them in the trash and mistakenly believed it was because she didn't like them. She was missing that nurturing gene imbedded in most women, it having whizzed by her DNA at top speed, a vacancy so grand that no baggie of powdered flower nutrients could save her.

It shouldn't have surprised her then to see such magnificence bloom in her absence. In fact, it made every sense in the world.

Po shot between her legs the instant she opened the door. Panic activated in her chest as he sprinted for the plant. What if it was poisonous? Dangerous? Some kind of mutant plant with sentient vines excited at the thought of a nice, puppy meal? Before she could crystalize a warning, he had already trotted up to the nearest tendril, extended it a haughty sniff, and pissed on it. He was back at her feet before she'd even said a word.

Again, she found herself leaning over the curious growth in her yard like a surgeon to a tumor, considering the best way to handle her predicament. It was vinelike, almost tropical in appearance. It certainly wasn't reminiscent of any other naturally growing plant in this area, most of which were of the pointy succulent variety. Curiouser and curiouser.

"What is this, Po?" she asked. His response was to march toward the door and demand to be let inside.

Josie tapped the perimeter of the growth with her foot—it sprung back into place with ease. Before joining Po, she snapped a picture with her phone, both for research purposes and for posterity. If it had bloomed this quickly in one day, what might it do in two? Or five? Or thirty?

She felt compelled to lock the door behind her as she started her day, always keeping a wary eye toward the yard. Then, she googled it for answers.

The results of her search revolved mostly around some grass types and a few flowering plants. Not at all what she was dealing with. So, then she tried 'Sonoran Vines,' which produced a list of varying desert flowers.

Josie searched the best she could for anything matching the ninja vine in her yard. Vampire flowers. Underground vines. Aggressive plants. The only plants that even came close to matching the description of the thing in her backyard were only found in the deep recesses of the Amazon.

Checking on it again, it seemed to have stalled its growth, as if too shy to do so under her watch. At the rate it had appeared, she assumed it must be writhing with newness at all hours of the day. Instead it was stagnant—as permanent to her yard as the brick wall surrounding the property.

But she'd have to deal with this thing later as it was time to get to work. She was already thirty minutes behind schedule, and as predicted, Jackie had indeed further inflamed his customer. It took ten minutes to formulate a response email for him to send to his customer, who was now threatening to not only sue him but go to the local news. Not that any news station would give two fucks about a minor billing dispute, but it was enough to send Jackie into aneurism territory, which was exactly the point of it. Josie knew from the outset this customer was going to get exactly what they wanted, even from Jackie, a person always gunning for a good fight, because at the end of the day the customer has only one person to focus on. The business owner has dozens/hundreds/thousands of moving pieces assaulting them throughout the day, and their willpower always gives out first. But she couldn't state so outright—Jackie had to come to that conclusion himself. He would eventually. And he would hate the hell out of it.

The morning zoomed by, she nearly forgot about the plant until it was time for her afternoon tea. Inspecting it through her kitchen window, it looked like it had spread somewhat, oozing like an oil spill.

While waiting for the water in the kettle to boil, she stepped outside to give the weed another look.

It consumed nearly a quarter of her yard now. At this rate, it'd be crawling up the sides of her house by dinner time. What began as a curiosity now bloomed into a sprawling dread in her gut. Things were getting out of hand—her day was completely thrown off. What if this plant never stopped growing? Would she have to call someone? Who do you call for things like this?

Excuse me, 911? I need someone to come handle this plant situation. No, I'm not injured, but I am quite cross. What do you mean this is not an emergency? Hello?

She resolved to handle this growth herself immediately. She grabbed the sharpest steak knife she owned, then donned rubber dish gloves and stormed into the yard prepared to slice the center stalk in the hopes of killing the whole beast. It seemed logical. Thorough. A decent enough plan to keep her mind at ease.

Turned out to be none of those things.

Leering over the plant, she considered her options—what if its sap is poisonous? Or its leaves? Or maybe it releases a toxic cloud as a defense?—and figuring an immediate poisoning was preferable to this stress, lowered herself to the ground and took her blade to the stalk. She hadn't so much as kissed the metal to the shoot when a noise vibrated throughout her body. An insistent, startling cough as if another person had appeared just over her and was trying to steal her attention.

She shot to her feet, dropping the knife to the ground, and swatting blindly in all directions. Someone was there—the noise was unmistakably human. She heard it. She *felt* it—felt it as if she'd been the one to make it. Felt it within her bone marrow. But as she spun about, thudding heart overwriting the rest of her senses, she found nothing but dirt and plants and Po scraping his tiny paw across the back door. Nothing frantic about the way he behaved—he just wanted to be let out. If there had been another person in the yard he'd have been snarling and squealing with such vigor the entire neighborhood would have heard him.

Happy for the company, she darted toward the door and let him out, hoping his heightened sense of smell and hearing might pick up on anything she would have missed.

But Po simply trotted to the edge of the patio, took a dump on the concrete, and lazily worked his way back toward the house.

A mindfuck was all it was. A record skip of the brain, like the sudden loud bangs that jolt her awake just as she was falling asleep at night. The noise was a misfire and nothing more.

Josie was more than happy to accept that notion and move about her day, but as she brushed her palm to the door handle the noise returned and graduated to a fully-fledged voice.

"You forgot your knife."

Josie froze. Po showed no indication that he had heard a thing. This was no brain trickery—this was a concise, spoken sentence. The words rang throughout her body. They sang inside her, something close and intimate. Nothing like the faraway voice of a stranger spoken across the yard. This was like an articulated thought, almost cartoonish as if someone was narrating a thought bubble over her head she didn't know was there.

In the face of such oddities, miracles, and wonders, people have varying responses. Josie imagined a slew of rational directions to take, including but not limited to screaming, running away, or firing a gun into the air—if she'd owned one, that is.

Instead, without turning away from the door, she said. "Excuse me?"

"I said you forgot your knife, although I don't know exactly what you wished to accomplish with a steak knife. It's so dull, it could barely butter bread."

"It's the only knife I had." Jesus fuck, what was she doing? Too terrified and confused to face her accuser, she found herself equally irritated at their boldness. The reflection of her glass window revealed nothing behind her. Shocking, considering the closeness of their voice.

"Well, you forgot it."

"So?"

"So, I figured you might want to come get it."

"If I wanted to come get it, I would have."

"You don't have to be afraid of me."

"I have every right to feel however the hell I want, thank—" Josie wheeled toward the yard, incensed, and immediately regretted the decision.

Squatting center in the yard, surrounded by the mystery vines, was her intruder.

A skeleton.

A Halloween decoration. A toy. A fake.

Josie considered this for a few seconds, gaping at it from her spot on the patio. A skeleton. This couldn't possibly be real.

"I am real, in case you're wondering."

The voice zippered up her spine, then down again so that her skin bubbled. But the skeleton didn't move—its mouth remained

19

clamped shut, its barely-there body as stiff as cardboard. Or bone.

This was completely fine.

"You read minds?"

"*People are predictable.*"

Definitely fine. "You do this often, do you?"

"*Depends on your definition of often.*"

Okay. Sure. "What are you?"

"*What do you think I am?*"

"A skeleton. That talks."

"*That sums it up nicely, I'd say.*"

"Nothing to add?"

"*Your description was sufficient.*"

Po tapped his untrimmed nails on the patio, dancing in anticipation of being let inside. If he noticed the skeleton there, he didn't seem perturbed by its presence. Josie wasn't sure what bothered her more—the fact that Po portrayed more unease toward a slight breeze than this inexplicable creature of myth, or the fact that he might not see anything at all.

"I'm going inside." Go inside. Drink her tea. Sit down. Go back to work. She had a day to finish, and by golly, she was going to no matter what this scientific aberration lingering in her yard had to say.

Perhaps she was suffering a mental breakdown. Maybe she needed a nap.

"*See you later.*"

The pique of the voice flourished a new wave of chills throughout her body. She believed the skeleton when they said they would 'see her later.'

Josie refused to look back as she fled inside her house, not sure if she was afraid of the skeleton still being there or of it not being there. Both options were bad. She was either crazy or she was talking to the dead. Either way, she was utterly fucked.

The kettle had shut off, leaving tepid tap water for her tea. Carefully avoiding the window, she refilled her mug and waited for the new pot to boil.

She didn't know what to do. How do people handle shit like this? How do they know if they are going insane?

In that moment, she did something she'd carefully avoided for many, many months—she thought of her dad. He'd been like her—a pragmatist and a debunker. Spirituality was not something either of them could subscribe to, and most of the time she didn't feel any worse for it because she was like him, and he was like her. And they weren't alone.

But now he was gone, and she *was* alone, and an apparition on her property was demanding her attention. A lot of moving parts to this delusion.

While her mind whirled, her motor functions kicked into high gear and prepared her tea.

What if this thing *was* her dad, coming back to haunt her?

The idea repulsed her so profoundly, she restrained the bile creeping up from her gut. No. He wouldn't do that. No.

But could he?

Unable to stop herself, she peered through the window overlooking the yard only to confirm the skeleton was still present. It hadn't budged. From where she stood, it looked like a bad practical joke, a prop meant to startle the next unwitting fool to cross its path. She thought if she watched long enough it might give something away to explain its presence. No footprints were leading to or away. There were no visible strings or props. She saw no wires or metal, nothing to maintain the squat position in which it waited. Shadows pooled discordant and chaotic, as the skeleton filtered the sunlight through its bones.

She was counting its fingers and toes for inhuman anomalies when her doorbell rang. Po bolted for the front door, both to cuss at the intruder and to avoid the tea and broken bits of ceramic as Josie's mug hit the tile. Her hands trembled. The doorbell had scared the shit out of her.

With Po snarling between her feet, she trudged to the door and looked through the peephole. The new neighbor stood there. Of course, this is when the lady decides to stop by. There wasn't ever a good time to stop by in Josie's opinion, but immediately after discovering a sentient, passive aggressive skeleton in her yard was probably one of the worst.

Josie wished she could pretend she wasn't home, but her car was parked in the driveway. Instead of taking a hint and leaving, though, she waited a few minutes and then rang the doorbell again.

The noise gave Po a new life, and he barked as if on fire. Fine. Josie flung open the door with such immediacy that anyone with sense would know that she'd been just on the other side. She prayed the puzzle pieces would fit together for this woman, so she'd understand the gravity of her intrusion.

"I'm so sorry to bother you," the woman said, the smile on her face suggesting she, in fact, wasn't sorry at all. "But I was wondering if you had a screwdriver."

The woman was disheveled and dirty as if she'd been tending a garden all morning. Dark fingermarks littered the front of her smock—a frumpy flowered thing that avoided her body as if allergic to it. Her frizzy hair was stamped to her head underneath a green sun visor.

Josie didn't miss a beat. "No." She wasn't even sure if that was true, but she wasn't about to tear her house apart looking for one for this lady who had already irritated her beyond measure.

"You *don't* have a screwdriver?"

"Neither do you. I don't see why that's so shocking."

"I just moved. It's lost in a box somewhere."

"I don't know what to tell you."

"Do you not have one or do you just not want to lend it to me?"

Exactly who was this woman? Josie's wispy patience all but evaporated, but that didn't bother the woman. Her smile creased the edges of her face in the same, easy way as if she'd just been handed a flower from a new suitor. "Ask next door. He fixes his truck sometimes. I bet he has a few."

The woman tilted her head to the side, considering, then shrugged. "I'll do that. What's his name? I don't want to be rude."

Josie's brows furrowed into another dimension, and the woman immediately corrected herself.

"Oh. I know your name. You're Josie, right? I found some of your mail on the ground." She produced a folded-up envelope from the pocket of her smock, not even bothering to smooth the creases. "Here."

Josie glared at the envelope, recognizing the value coupon logo on the front—junk mail which usually bypassed her kitchen table altogether and landed directly in the recycle bin. "And who are you?" she asked, plucking her mail from the woman's dusty fingers.

"I'm Sue, your new neighbor."

To Josie's eternal appreciation, Sue did not bother to extend a hand.

"His name is Max," Josie said. "Or Matt. I don't know. I'm pretty sure it starts with an M. Anyway, welcome to the neighborhood and all that."

"Good to meet you, Josie," she said.

Josie detected nothing but pure sincerity in Sue's voice, even as she shut the door in her face, and such earnestness made Josie feel like a moldy sponge. She hated feeling like a sponge. It was her job, her self-made career, to make everyone else the sponge. And here she was making a gigantic ass of herself.

Po, unperturbed by human social constructs, wagged his tail

as she faced him. So what if she was awkward? The woman—Sue—wouldn't be here long anyway. Besides, this was the absolute least of her current worries. This exchange wasn't anything to agonize over, considering the circumstances. So, it was fine.

Totally fine.

"What I should have said was—I should have introduced myself after she asked for Mike's name. That's what I should have done. Something like, 'I'm Josie by the way.' She already knew my name, but she also would have known that I wouldn't have known that, you know what I mean? You don't know what I mean. You're a dog."

Work ended at five and she'd been three sheets to the wind ever since. The skeleton was gone. As soon as Sue had left, she checked the yard and found it empty of all paranormal machinations. The weeds were still there, but they presented less of a concern to her at this time, and she deduced she could deal with those if she had to. Her plan—half-cocked and swimming in vodka shots—was to ignore them completely. The abandoned steak knife would have to make do with its new home, forage a new life in the wilderness. She figured if she left the plants alone, the skeleton wouldn't come back and she could go on living her regular, thrilling life.

Po was less enthused, having been denied access to the yard and having to settle for the puppy pads she had drunkenly strewn throughout the house on which to relieve himself. Josie loudly explained to him that peeing indoors was for his own good. He whined incessantly for two hours before giving up and sulking on his favorite couch pillow.

Night poured over her house profoundly enough to obscure all but the outermost edges of the plants. For all she knew the skeleton had returned and was spying on her from the cover of darkness, taking notes, spare pencil behind the hypothetical ear, newsie hat propped on its bald skull. Or it lurked, salivating over her ignorance, preparing a dastardly ambush for the minute she fell asleep. She imagined smooth fingers encircling the doorknob of the backdoor, the pop and clack of bones against the tile of the hallway, the emptiness of sound as it slid over her sleeping body, considering what to do with her.

But then … no. The thing gave off a distinct aura of a smart ass, more the type to get bored by the macabre. Too ancient to adhere to cheap tropes.

"Maybe I should show Sue my skeleton! That ought to keep her away. Unless she's into weird shit like that. Then, God, it could be worse. I could wake up and find *her* in my bedroom instead of the skeleton. Jesus, Po, can you imagine?"

Po turned his buggy eyes toward her without lifting his head—for a dog so enamored with his owner, this was his firmest form of resistance.

She poured another shot. Her last shot—yes, definitely— and joined Po on the couch. He immediately crawled onto her lap, unleashing his disdain at the events of the day in a series of exasperated whimpers. He was a slow leaking balloon.

Josie swung him into a hug, of which he immediately balked, but she couldn't stand to look into his sad, pathetic eyes anymore. He was a good dog and didn't deserve to be trapped inside the house with an owner suffocating within a fog of booze vapor. He deserved to have a nice yard in which to haughtily trot and an owner who took him on regular walks.

"But you're stuck with me, aren't you, Po?" He placed his muzzle in the comfortable place between her breasts, eyes closing as she caressed the ends of his ears, a comfort for them both. Before long, Po had slipped into a deep sleep, dreaming in puppy. His jaw trembled as he chased imaginary mice, his paws twitched through the throes of REM. Josie took immense comfort knowing that this little creature felt safe enough with her to dream, to completely let go of all consciousness. He trusted her. Probably not a wise move but she was grateful all the same.

Tomorrow she would get to the bottom of this. She would take Po for a walk like she always meant to. Get outside. See something other than the empty walls of her own house. They both could use some fresh air. She'd dump her booze down the drain, stop this alcohol-fused delusion of talking skeletons. She would be fine.

The skeleton was gone now. She just had to keep it that way.

DAY THREE

THE SKELETON WAS not gone.

Po thrashed his paws at the backdoor. Bleary from a fitful night's sleep, she unthinkingly opened the door to let him out, remembering too late why she'd locked him inside. He darted for the farthest corner of the patio, twirling like a top until his bladder and bowels could no longer contain themselves. Only then did she lock eye sockets with the skeleton.

The sight of the uninvited bony guest turned her skin to ice, shock slamming into her shaky morning body with full force. Fuck.

It stared right at her, though she'd yet to notice any movement.

"Good morning, Little Bird."

Josie looked over her shoulder, expecting to see whoever the skeleton referred to as 'Little Bird.' There was no one.

"Who are you talking to?"

"You."

"That's not my name."

"It is what I have decided to call you."

"But that isn't my name."

"Does it upset you?"

Josie considered it. As far as nicknames go, this was rather innocent. She'd been called worse—by her ex, by her ex-friends that favored her ex, shit, by her mother, too. And there was something to be said about this creature not knowing her name.

"I guess it's fine."

"Excellent."

The plants had maneuvered themselves during the night, stretching out in a star pattern to the farthest corners of her property. The skeleton remained at their center, cross-legged with bony hands resting on each kneecap.

Po joined her on the patio, sitting his chihuahua butt on top of her foot.

"What are you?" she asked the skeleton.

"*A skeleton.*"

"Yes, I can see that."

"*So, why did you ask?*"

"Skeleton's don't usually reanimate and stalk strangers on their property."

"*True.*"

"So, what are you?"

"*I already told you.*"

"You know what I mean."

"*I'm afraid I do not.*"

"Really?" Josie was all sorts of cross. She was knotted up in crossness. This thing was not only uninvited but was also a sarcastic asshole. "You mean to tell me that you really have *no idea* what I'm asking?"

"*Perhaps you should rethink your question.*"

"Where did you come from?"

"*Your yard.*"

"Why are you here?"

"*To talk.*"

"To me?"

"*To you.*"

"Why?"

"*Because you're interesting.*"

Josie scoffed. She didn't mean to, but the burst of air through her nostrils couldn't be tamed. Her, interesting? That was a fantastical laugh if she'd ever heard one. She imagined what her ex would say about that, considering one of his primary complaints in their marriage was her absolute refusal to conform to the dream life he'd always envisioned for the two of them. The mere thought set her nerves on edge, hitting a mental block she'd thrown up two years ago, one so aggressive and imposing that the skeleton in the yard was a far more comfortable topic.

"I think you're mistaken."

"*I don't often make mistakes.*"

"Talking isn't really my thing."

"*So I've gathered.*"

"*So*, I don't know what you're expecting."

"*My expectations are low, believe me.*"

"Then why are you here? Just go away and find someone else to play with." She considered after the words had left her that this may not be wise. Who knew what this thing could do once offended? How does one offend a skeleton anyway?

Feet planted on the pavement, Josie awaited the response, an arsenal of rebuttals bouncing against her teeth just itching to spring loose.

But the skeleton said nothing. They remained for so long Josie's annoyance slipped into confusion. She felt drunk—well, she probably was still a bit drunk. She needed some coffee. It was too early for this nonsense without coffee.

"I need caffeine," she said eventually.

"*Don't let me stop you.*"

"I'd offer you some, but—" She gesticulated toward the skeleton. "You know."

"*I appreciate the offer.*"

"Does that mean you want some or you just … never mind. No, you don't want any. Right?"

"*Right, but thanks.*"

"I've never done this before."

"*Made coffee?*"

"No."

"*Entertained?*"

"The skeleton part. Whatever you are."

"*That's to be expected.*"

"Okay. Well, bye." Josie fled inside the house, spending a solid ten minutes gaping out her window at the skeleton. It did not disappear; did not move. Only waited. And waited. Po had already curled onto his chair cushion and settled in for a day of work. The distractions of yesterday and today meant her inbox was likely bursting. Josie didn't experience delays—her clients relied on that. Since her company's inception, she never had anything interfere with her life like this—she'd cultivated the exact sort of existence to ensure no interruptions. One bad day and she could lose hundreds of dollars in a snap, hundreds she could not afford.

"Hey," she said at the closed window. "Can you hear me in here?"

The skeleton did not indicate that it could.

"If you can hear me, wave a hand. I don't know, nod, or something."

Nothing

She cracked open the door. "Hey, uh, skeleton thing. I have to get to work."

"*Don't worry about me.*"

Its voice permeated every molecule of her body, despite the door being cracked a half an inch. She snapped the door shut.

"I don't think it can hear me in here, Po."

Po snored, paws twitching.

"That's good. I think that's good. Is that good? I don't know."

Whether the small privacy was good or not, it would have

to do. With that, her internal business switch was flipped. She banged the espresso machine, heated the kettle, prepared her morning ibuprofen, and turned on her laptop. Skeleton or no skeleton, she had shit to do.

As it turned out, she had little trouble tuning out all recent anomalies once her inbox populated. If anything, the swell of requests set her at ease—this, she could handle. Here, she was in her element.

Professionalism oozed from her pores.

She was doing fine—a working, functioning human who was fine. Po wriggled, ready for his treat, and she used the opportunity to stretch her legs, which was fine, absolutely and perfectly normal and fine. Then, she made tea like any other perfectly normal day, took more pain meds like any other regular, uneventful, and boring day, only to then gaze gloomily at her— surprise!—skeleton friend. Josie.exe had crashed.

Scattering a few milk bones on the kitchen floor, Josie propped open the door again.

"You're still here."

"*Still here.*"

"I was hoping, you know, you wouldn't be."

"*Sorry to disappoint.*"

"Any thoughts on when you will be leaving?"

"*Many.*"

"Care to extrapolate?"

"*You haven't even asked my name.*"

"Excuse me?"

"*You haven't once asked how to address me.*"

Flummoxed, Josie loosened her protective grip on the door so Po was able to nudge it open and blow past her.

"I don't recall inviting you here to begin with."

"*Odd.*"

Josie elbowed the door the rest of the way so it swung against the wall. "You have some nerve infesting my yard like this and calling *me* odd."

"*I call 'em how I see 'em.*"

"So, what's your name, then?"

"*I don't want to tell you now.*"

"Then leave." She waved the skeleton away like a bad stench. "And take your weird plants with you."

"*I'm afraid it isn't that simple.*"

"And why is that?"

"*Because they are not ready to leave.*"

With those words said, the vines lifted off the dirt, rearing like pissed off cobras. Josie backed into her table trying to get away as dirt billowed from the disturbance, quickly obscuring the skeleton from sight. Vines whipped themselves around the patio supports, strangling the wooden beams.

Then, the unusual attack stopped. The vines lay docile, frozen like waves clawing up the back of her house. The skeleton sat unfazed, coated in a new layer of dust.

"*See what I mean?*"

Po was furious, positively enraged by the rudeness of the outburst. His panicked bark could shatter windows.

"What the fuck are those things?"

"*Annoyed, I think. It's difficult to tell.*"

Josie shaded her eyes despite the darkness, an act in the same vein as turning down the radio in the car when lost. The action alone helped to tamp down her anxiety. "You aren't controlling them?"

"*No more than how you control your dog. It's a kinship, like sisters.*"

"That's not particularly encouraging." Welts formed from Po's claws as he desperately dragged himself along her body. She picked him up, petting him until his eyelids pulled back.

34

"*He's a bad example.*"

"What do you want? What are you—they?—hoping to gain by terrifying me and my dog?"

"*I told you, I want to talk.*"

"Well, I don't want to fucking talk to you. I want you to get the hell off my property. I want you to go away. I'm tired."

"*You're frightened.*"

"Look what you did to my yard!" Po had downgraded to a skin-on-fire squeal, which was somehow worse than straight up howling.

"*Forgive me, which pile of dirt would you like me to restore?*"

"Fuck you, you ... Okay, what is your name?"

"*Now you want to know?*"

"It's finally a pertinent question."

"*You can call me Skelly.*"

"Skelly. Skelly the skeleton. Are you screwing with me?"

"*It has a nice flow.*"

"And what are your pronouns? She? He? Them?"

"*She is fine.*"

"Good to know. Well, on that note, fuck you, Skelly."

"*Charming.*"

Josie slammed the door behind her, leaving the vines and the bones and the dust to settle themselves.

DAY FOUR

THE CURTAINS WERE drawn. She'd pinned a sheet to the drywall above the backdoor with thumbtacks and a single loose nail she'd found in her junk drawer. Josie hadn't dared pull them back, even to peek. She was on lockdown. This was not a drill.

Skelly said she wanted to talk. Well, Skelly could wait her happy ass outside. Josie was not one to be broken so easily, nor one to force to talk when she wasn't in the mood for talking. Ask her mother. Or her ex. Hell, ask her therapist, whatever her name was—Lowenstein? Or was it Zweig? Josie had learned a thing a two from all her failures, the primary of which being that she had no equal in disintegrating friendly relationships. In this matter, she had no equal.

Josie took explicit care to avoid the windows and doors of her house. Food and alcohol were both getting perilously low, so today she would feast on old graham crackers, questionable yogurt only a week or so past the expiration date, while carefully rationing her four remaining bottles of vodka. Wednesday was usually her grocery delivery day, but she'd canceled the order on account of Skelly, terrified by the idea of her ethereal booming voice scaring away Josie's regular delivery guy. And she liked Kevin. He was a good kid that didn't once open his mouth in her presence aside from a quick greeting and hints on which alcohol might be on sale next week, and she tipped him well for the courtesy.

This also meant that Po was once again reduced to using puppy pads, and although he complained much less than before, he still anxiously trotted from pad to pad.

"We're going to get through this, buddy," she said, for both their benefit. "We've got this."

They'd settled in, she at her computer and Po on his chair when someone knocked on the door. At first, she imagined Skelly standing there, irritated at being shut out, making a scene on her front porch. The idea crystallized so thoroughly she forced herself a glance to the yard. Skelly's form jutted out of the ground like a gargoyle, just as stoic and mundane as expected.

There was another knock, and Skelly hadn't moved. Shit.

Josie decided to ignore it. She shouted at Po to get away from the door, loud enough that anyone knocking would hear and hopefully understand she was willfully ignoring them. Instead of abiding the quiet lesson Josie dished out, the knocker upgraded to ringing the doorbell.

Squinting through the peephole, Josie understood why. Sue was why.

She propped her door open just enough in which to slide a single piece of mail. "I'm a bit busy at the moment," she said.

"I understand, but I thought you might want to be aware of this." She spoke with an unflappable calm, which was infinitely more alarming than the kooky flightiness of their first encounter. Josie's thoughts immediately went to Skelly.

She opened the door a little wider. "Aware of what?"

"Come see." And without another gesture, Sue cut across Josie's yard to the small space separating their properties.

"Just tell me, Sue," Josie shouted as the woman disappeared around the corner. "Sue?"

But Sue was either out of earshot or ignoring her. "Sue!"

Damn it. Damn this woman. If Josie shut the door now, Sue would come back and they'd have to repeat this entire process. What kind of fresh, purgatory bullshit was this?

Pushing Po back with a foot, she slipped out the front and followed Sue, finding her knelt by the stucco on the side of her house, pointing at the wall.

"What is it?" Josie asked, seeing nothing of any importance.

Sue pointed again. "See this?"

"I don't see anything." Fear clawed at Josie the instant she spoke, imagining Sue getting far too close. Maybe popping her nose over the fence. Maybe spotting those vines and getting curious. From Josie's perspective nothing appeared amiss, but who knew what Sue had already seen?

"Termites."

"What?"

"Termites."

"What?"

They might have continued this a few more rounds had Sue not aggressively indicated toward the rust-colored termite tube just peeking out of the wall. "Termites."

"Oh, that's it?"

"My house has dozens of them."

"So, you decided to inspect mine, too?"

"I happened to run across it while I was taking pictures for the landlord."

"Why were you taking pictures for the landlord?"

"So he can fix them."

Josie snorted. "Good luck with that."

But Sue was unperturbed. "I just thought you'd like to know that you have them, too."

"You could have just told me. It wasn't necessary to drag me outside as if I'd never seen a termite tube before. Especially living here." She gestured toward Sue's rental.

Sue straightened her fanny pack. "You don't get out much, do you?"

"What business is that of yours?"

"Do you drink tea?"

The sudden misdirection threw off all her irritated momentum. Her arsenal of insults piled up, things aflame and smoking, as her brain tried to catch up.

"I have all this tea and never anyone to share it with. You should come over for tea."

No, no, Josie did not want to go over for tea. She did not want to engage in small talk with Sue. Nor did she want to be trapped inside that house. She did not want to be invited over again and again. She did not want any of Sue's cheap tea.

"That's okay, Sue. Thanks for the offer."

"You don't like tea?"

"No, it's not—"

"Coffee then. I have cookies."

"I'm fine. Really."

"I see. You don't want to come over."

What a power play. Making Josie be the jerk and admit aloud what both clearly already knew. Well, two could play at that game.

"No, Sue. I really don't." Fine. She wanted Josie to be the mean one. Well, fine. She had a little too much going on right now to care about what some temporary neighbor thought of her.

Instead of feigning dismay or offense, Sue simply patted the top of Josie's hand and said, "Then we shall make it very quick."

Fuuuuuuuuuuuuuuuuuuuuuuuuuuuuuuuuuuuck.

Josie watched her go, miffed as hell yet struggling to protest.

"How about Saturday? One o'clock. You seem like a late riser. I'll have tea, coffee, and treats. I promise not to keep you longer than twenty minutes."

"Why are you so insistent? I've made it clear that I have no interest in coming."

Sue stopped, considering. "If you come, I promise never again to speak to you for as long as I am your neighbor. Unless you instruct otherwise."

Sue did not wait for a response. She'd played her final hand and it'd landed just as she expected. In the few days since she'd moved in, Sue had already bothered her more than her other neighbors had in the past year. This was not an offer Josie would dare turn down.

"Fine. Twenty minutes. That's it."

"I'll set a timer if that would make you feel more at ease."

"It would."

Sue had reached her door, pausing as her hand grazed the handle. "Oh, yeah, you might want to call a landscaper, too. Those vines in your yard are getting a little out of control."

Adrenaline surged through her body, tinnitus blotting out anything else Sue might have said. "What are you talking about?"

"They're curling over the top of our shared fence. I hope you get a handle on them as I wouldn't want them to interfere with the garden I'm planting."

Skelly. That bitch.

Josie didn't respond, instead she issued a quick goodbye before tearing through her house toward the backdoor, and then through it. She stopped just shy of the patio's edge.

The vines had spread.

What began as an outbreak in the middle of the yard had become an infestation of divine proportions—vines coated the dirt like a blanket, a frozen sea of twisting green tendrils, some as thick as a garden hose. They suffocated the struts and pillars of her patio, crashing over the edge of the concrete, and spilling languidly over the cool gray. Her fence was all but invisible—vines choked out the sight of the brick, replacing its utilitarian appeal with a botanist's fever dream. Colorful buds of pink, yellow, and orange aggressively dotted the thicker strands. Nothing remained of her bland, neglected lot.

In the center of it all, resting comfortably on a throne of tall stalks, was Skelly. Leg perched over one knee, she rested the side of her skull against an open palm. If she possessed skin or muscle or a face, Josie could swear it would have been shaped into a malicious grin.

"*Good morning, Little Bird.*"

"What have you done?"

"*Do you like it?*"

"No, I don't. I hate it. Stop."

"*Stop what?*"

"Stop … this! The neighbors are asking about it now."

"*So.*"

"So?" Josie was stumped. Surely this creature must understand the problem at hand. In fact, Josie would wager her entire business on that fact. "You know exactly what you're doing."

"*You don't evolve into an immortal skeleton without understanding a thing or two about power dynamics.*"

Bold. Too bold. Josie was outmatched. And she was thoroughly pissed off about it. "Can you at least get that shit away from the fences?"

"*Sure I could.*"

Josie waited. Nothing happened. "*Will* you?"

"*I will.*"

Still nothing. Po sniffed around the new yard, circling Skelly as if she were nothing more than a new pile of dirt. He peed, then stalked back inside, waiting for Josie in his usual place beside her at the kitchen table.

"Will you do it now?"

"*No.*"

42

Josie clawed at her face, willing everything to just stop—for Skelly to just go away and leave her alone. Her very molecules trembled with frustration, a scream welling up from some recessed part of her soul. She was hot and short of breath and teetering dangerously on the cusp of an unrecoverable panic attack when a tickling sensation spun around her ankles and up her calves. Vines.

She tried to yank away but was cemented in place by their vise grip, toppling over backward, skull plummeting toward imminent pain. But it never came. They caught her just before she hit the ground.

Josie flailed pathetically. "What was that?"

Vines surged upward, propping her onto her feet before releasing her. Skelly had assumed a new position, now upright and alert on her throne.

"*Interesting.*"

The vines went slack at Josie's feet. "What are these things?"

"*Simple vines.*"

"Cut the bullshit. I've never seen a vine move like this before."

"*That doesn't mean they haven't.*"

"No one has ever seen a vine move like that."

"*You have.*"

"Excluding now, obviously."

"*And you're awfully assertive about it, considering.*"

"So, you're telling me there are rogue vines around the world, writhing like snakes and preventing minor injuries?" Josie scanned the yard, searching for more movement. The vines lay flat and dumb like any other plant. Nothing at all to indicate what they had just done. Nothing to indicate whether Josie was delirious.

"*All I'm saying is that it's possible.*"

"Then, what are they? What do they want?" Curiosity muted her frustration—she genuinely wanted to know.

Kneeling, she ran her fingers across the top of a thicker vine, one just recently tethered to her ankle. It plopped lifelessly to the ground when dropped.

"*Would you like to hear a story?*"

Josie froze, caught off guard by the question. Somehow this felt like a trap—Skelly's way to wrangle her into a horrifying situation well outside Josie's comfort zone. But she was captivated by these vines now and weighed her responses on her metaphorical scale.

- No It's a trap
- Yes
- It's a trap, but with possible information
- What kind of story?
- It's a trap, executed after a long monolog and potential embarrassment
- Ignore, go inside
- It's a trap, Skelly unleashes the vines on the neighborhood

"I feel like I'm fucked no matter what I say."

"*Good! You're learning.*"

"I might as well be entertained then."

"*That's the spirit.*"

The ground began to move. Vines lurched and slithered and whipped to their places. Within seconds both her familiar yard and Skelly along with it, were gone, replaced with a writhing knot of vines that circled Josie. For a moment, she was certain she was about to be killed, suffocated inside a cocoon of terrible miracles. The recluse lost inside the jungle of her lonely home. Or more likely, Skelly and the vines would leave. They'd find her alone, her death mask wide-eyed and horrified, Po nibbling on her ears for sustenance. She imagined her mother being interviewed. "I told her to come to the boat. The toilets are finally working. Now I have two toilets and no daughter to share them with." She imagined a wail, baffling and destructive, ripping her soul at its seams.

But as she imagined these things, a small light filtered through the thick dark of the vines, Skelly's voice booming through her body like a subwoofer.

"*There are corpses trapped in the sea—so far below that human hands could never reach them. They were trapped long ago.*"

The vines undulated uncomfortably, mimicking the surge of waves.

"*The beings fell from the sky and landed in the vast oceans of Earth. They were creatures of light, and they drowned.*"

Josie felt compelled to chime in. "Angels. You're talking about angels." But while the words formed on her lips, no noise emerged. She was strangled by the depth, by the pressure of the deep. The vines raged, and a new sort of terror gripped her—the terror of imminent drowning. Skelly was killing her.

"*They drowned, waterlogged and heavy, but did not die. Instead, they survived at the bottom of the sea, deprived of light, shadowed, anemic, and sunk.*"

The vines surged outward, oozing away from her, encasing her in a much larger, but no less dark and dreary, cocoon. Josie couldn't see beyond her outstretched fingers.

"*They ached for the light, and envoys were deployed to the surface. Those chosen, brave few would make for their homeland, their light, and would return to their fellows once a safe path was ensured. This was the only way, lest they risk the entirety of their species.*"

Josie saw them—just enough out of sight that they formed no more than sinewy strings. There was a group, a gathering of things. A few lonely strands broke away, wriggling with conviction upward before they disappeared.

"*Those envoys never returned. Many speculated on their fate, none of these speculations nearing the truth. The pragmatists among them built a life on the seafloor. A new generation was born, and another after that, each generation changed from their parents. Evolved. Mutated. Monsters. Gifts.*"

Movement jostled her attention. Creatures parted away from the darkness, pieces of them wafting through a broken horizon, partially obscured by what Josie could only describe as a curtain of tall seaweed. None ever ventured close, but the familiarity of their forms was striking—lean, vertical, with one head and four limbs. They were humanoid, but most certainly not human.

"*The beings traded flesh for rot, their air bodies unsuited for the compressive sea. Water pounded them, flattened them to a pulp, and even so they survived, their bodies massacred along with their ancestry. But they had story and myth. The final vestiges of their people clung together by their tongues alone, refusing to die.*

Until they became nothing, and in their nothingness were once again granted wings. Like motes of dust, they began to float."

Darkness encapsulated her wholly. There was nothing to see, nothing but the spots in her vision against a sightless curtain. It was so thoroughly disorienting that within seconds Josie had lost track of all direction, a sensation of weightlessness turning her insides into soup.

"*The remaining pieces of their beinghood held together at a molecular level, small, shaky atoms buzzing around in search of purpose. They rose and spread, whisked away by the currents of a deep, angry sea. But this did not destroy them—they billowed like smoke, bigger and bigger, unstoppable to even the barrier of the frozen corpses of the ones before them. Weaving between bodies, they called to the souls still present and incorporated them into their swelling storm.*

What one felt, the rest felt. What one saw, the others saw. Memories and language and pain and glory and dreams—all tumbled into one another, becoming an electrified, incorporeal mist.

After a millennium of water and ghosts, they rose, an army of corpses littering their wake. Then, they surfaced."

In an instant, the vines dropped away. She was back in her yard. The fear she should have felt throughout the entire exchange slammed into her at once. Nested within now limp vines, Josie thrashed them off her. Never in her life had she experienced such a primal desire to flee.

Skelly reflected on the scene impassively.

Free of the vines' grip, she scrambled as far away from them as she could, which so happened to be the section of fence she shared with Sue, now conveniently empty of vines.

"Get away from me," she said, although not all the words made it out of her mouth coherently. She found it ironic that the moment the vines were removed she prayed for someone else— anyone else—to notice them. Things were getting a little too wild for her liking, and this was usually the time that she faded into the bushes and let another human handle it.

But today no other humans were watching. It was just her and Skelly and Po and—

"Po, no! No! Get inside! Get!" The dog tottered toward the pile of vines. For a thing so hellbent on growling the wind into submission, he was awfully cavalier about magic vines that could literally strangle him in a second. "Pogoddamnitgetawayfromthere—"

"Calm down. They will not injure your dog."

"Don't tell me to calm down. Po! *Po!*" Sprinting was not an activity in which she often participated, excepting for life and death situations, so as she pressed her feet to the ground to save her dog, she immediately pulled a calf muscle and tripped.

Vines shuffled before her, then out of sight in an unrelenting whirl of movement. A path cleared between her and Po, and he cantered toward her like a fancy horse.

"*Get it together, Little Bird.*"

Dog in hand, Josie clamored to her feet again. "If you ever touch me again, I will burn your vines to the ground. You had no right to place those … things near me. You have no right to be here. Just get out of here and leave us alone."

Tears stroked her cheeks, hot and uncomfortable. This was a thing she spent at least fifty to seventy-five percent of her energy on preventing. She hated to cry, and now Skelly and her monster plants had brought forth the tears, while *outside* of all places.

Skelly said nothing else as Josie limped back inside the house, slamming the door shut with such gusto a frame in the living room fell off the wall.

Josie knew what frame had been destroyed the second she heard glass shattering. There weren't any others adorning her walls, save the one with a photo of her and her dad sitting at the helm of their very first boat. She was five and furiously tugging at the orange life vest looped around her neck. Her dad had put up a hand to block the shot, but Ma was quick on the trigger. What remained of his expression was both curmudgeonly and mirthful, his cinnamon-shaded hair dripping down the sides of his cheeks in sideburns he regretted from the day he shaved them until the day of his death.

It was a cheap frame that insisted on being replaced every so often, which Josie obliged by choosing the most obnoxious offering available at whichever thrift store she perused. The one before this had been made for a larger photo, an eight by ten inch, and she'd carefully placed the tiny three by five wallet photos in the center of it. The top of the frame read, "Life, Love, Happiness" in swirling, pretentious cursive. It had been a running joke between her and her dad ever since she first moved out and he'd gifted it to her in a frame he'd made from the cardboard his new television had come in. Her dad's reaction upon seeing the frame in which it currently resided, which was shortly before he'd gotten sick, was that it was the worst frame of them all. When he thought she wasn't looking, though, she'd caught him gazing intently at it as if to drag the visions of their younger selves into the palm of his hands for safekeeping.

And now it was broken.

Rescuing the photo, she plucked the larger pieces of glass from the floor, managing to cut herself several times. The broom was out back—she'd swept the patio after a dust storm last week and forgotten to bring it in. She didn't own a vacuum, and Po kept nosing around the spill site like an eager paparazzi.

Due to canceling her grocery delivery, she also found herself out of paper towels and napkins and any other cleaning item she might utilize in place of a broom. It had never occurred to her she might even need a handheld vacuum until now, and while cursing vigorously she mentally added one to her shopping list.

She tried blocking the area off with a chair and some books, but this only made Po more curious, and more insistent. She couldn't keep him away from the area all night, and it would be just their luck that he might get a shard stuck in his paw. Then they'd have to go to the vet or else the cut might get infected. She'd then be spending money she didn't have.

Shit. She needed the broom.

Skelly hadn't moved, but Josie shivered at the sight of the skeleton, a sensation of watchfulness tugging at the hairs on her arms. The feeling couldn't be articulated if she tried, something like a vibration or a tremor but without the shaking. A buzz without the buzz. But there was something to be said about Skelly's fixed attention, and she was certain that she held it now—each of them staring down the other, willing the other to break first.

This was no battle Josie could possibly win, an assertion they both knew for a fact. Josie had no cards at all, which was why the entire affair inflamed her so much. It wasn't just the intrusion, the antagonizing, the patronizing, and the weirdness, but more at the bone of it was her complete inability to refuse this interaction. Skelly clearly had all the time in the world.

Josie's only playable move was to die, which was no win either, what with being dead and all. And she did not want to die. Who would take care of Po?

This brought her back to the task at hand—retrieving her broom which rested against the house on the far side of the patio, separated by the still limp mound of vines. She'd either have to climb over the vines or go around them—in closer proximity to Skelly—to reach it. Both were inconvenient options. Both made her stomach lurch.

Po knocked down yet another book meant to keep him away from the glass and she knew she had no choice. If someone had to suffer, it sure as fuck wasn't going to be him. She stepped onto the patio, shouting at Skelly before she had the opportunity to open her metaphorical mouth.

"I just need the broom."

"*No one is stopping you.*"

"Don't act like your presence isn't a threat." Her rage resurfaced, coating her every remark.

"*It's an aggressive maneuver, I'll give you that, but desperate times call for desperate measures.*"

"Can't say I'm surprised. Desperation is usually what brings people to my doorstep." She tested the vines with her shoe, considering her options. They obeyed natural law and kept still. "Yet I wonder what a thing like you has to be desperate about.

50

And what you think you'll find in my shitty little house to cure it."

"*I am not desperate for myself, Little Bird. I am desperate for you.*"

She wasn't entirely processing Skelly's words as she slowly scaled the vines, her proximity to the broom being her only concern. "That so?"

"*Yes.*"

"That's stupid."

"*Is it?*"

"Completely." Reaching the red handle, she snatched the broom from the wall and ran the other way, adrenaline piqued and pumping. Pausing at the door, she finally considered what Skelly had said. "Why would you give a shit about me?"

"*Is there a reason I shouldn't?*"

"Probably. Plenty, I'm sure." If Skelly needed more data, there were plenty of people Josie could call upon to provide it.

"*Tell me Little Bird, what is it that you want?*"

"What do mean, what do I want? That's a nonsense question."

"*There must be some one thing that you desire above all else. You don't have to tell me, by the way. Just think about it.*"

"Are you some kind of genie itching to grant a few wishes?"

"*I would laugh, but I find the act doesn't translate well in this form.*"

"Then what do you care what my one desire is?"

"*I don't, really, but you should.*"

"Fine. What I really want is for you to get off my lawn and go back to wherever you came from. I want you to leave me alone. I want things to go back to how they were a few days ago. I want your plants gone. And I want my nice picture frame back."

"*That's more like four things rather than one, but I'll tell you what—I'll cut you a deal. Tell me a story, one only you can tell, one I've never heard before. Once you do, I will leave and never return if*" *that is your wish.*"

"And if I refuse?"

"*That is your decision, but it's a stupid one.*"

"Why do you care about my stories anyway?"

"*Call it boredom. Restlessness, perhaps. Anyway, do we have a deal?*"

Since her appearance, Skelly hadn't moved in Josie's presence. She simply manifested, frozen in position and shouting inside Josie's skull. At this pronouncement, Skelly's bony hand peeled away from her cheek and extended in the unmistakable form of a handshake.

Josie leaned into the broom as if a tether to her former life—a life where she swept up after storms and paid bills and slept with Po on the couch. She still had to do all these things, but now with this new, infuriating feature that refused to be ignored. "What's the catch? There's always a catch in situations like this."

"*I forgot to mention the catch, didn't I?*"

"Conveniently, yes."

"*It's not a catch, more like a stipulation.*"

"Okay."

"*You only have three days.*"

"Why three days?"

"*You were the one concerned with expediency. I thought this would please you.*"

"I prefer expediency on my own terms, thank you." Three days to spin a tale never yet heard by the likes of an apparently immortal being. This was fine.

"*As do we all, Little Bird, but the cosmos cares little for our petty desires.*"

"You strike me as the type who has a little more control of their destiny than most."

"*A long life can spare you many ills, but absolute autonomy is nigh impossible. At least as far as I'm concerned."*

Po was panting against the glass, fascinated by the exchange. It occurred to her then that she never clarified the terms. "And what happens if I fail?"

Skelly paused only a moment.

"The same thing that would happen to you at the end of these three days had I never arrived."

"That is ... chillingly vague."

"It should be."

"I think I deserve to know what happens at the end of these three days, Skelly."

"What you think you deserve and what you actually deserve often don't align, Little Bird."

"So, let me get this straight—you show up here, uninvited I might add, harass me and my dog, demanding bargains where I either win my freedom from you or suffer whichever consequences suit your whims, consequences that shall remain unnamed until prescribed. Do I have that correct so far?"

"No."

"No?"

"Not even remotely."

Josie rapidly tapped her index finger to her palm as she spoke. "Tell me where I'm wrong."

"For starters, I don't recall ever harassing your dog."

This was getting tiring. What Skelly proposed was too weighty a decision considering her current condition—a hair's breadth away from psychological collapse. Her hands and forehead were slick with sweat, and her stomach was nearing a full-scale revolt having not eaten a proper meal since the previous morning. As she stood there, every piece of her body prepared its exit strategy.

"What if I don't trust you?" she said.

"In that case, we both know that I'll be the last one to change your mind, but if you'll consider the fact that I haven't yet destroyed you, I think you'll begin to understand what I'm about."

An absurd notion Josie rebuked like expired fish, yet it had a ring of familiarity to it that she couldn't quite put away. Was Skelly that much different from any of her other human relationships of late? If she thought about it, her relationship with a skeleton might even be a cut above most. Skelly was leagues more receptive to conversation than any of her clients, and if Josie could handle the fragrant bouquet that was humanity and still turn a profit, then maybe she could handle Skelly just the same.

"My arm is getting tired."

"How so? You have no muscles."

"It's a figure of speech."

"Fine."

"Fine what?"

"Fine, we have a deal."

"Shake on it."

While Josie should have had every expectation of this inevitability, what with Skelly's outstretched hand and all, the sudden thought of touching her presented more pause than signing away her soul—or whatever just transpired, it was difficult to tell. Her hesitance was clearly apparent.

"I won't bite."

"Biting is the least of my worries."

"Then I'll be more specific. I, nor the vines, shall touch you in any way aside from the barest contact necessary to form a handshake."

Josie was not comforted by this, but it would have to do. Every molecule of her body rebelling, she somehow found the strength to hurl one foot in front of the other toward Skelly. Until then, she'd only communicated with her from whichever space was farthest away yet still within view. Actively approaching

Skelly felt like a defeat, as if she was beholden to her now. Which, she was.

The situation was thoroughly unnerving.

And if she'd hoped to glean any new information via their proximity, she found herself disappointed. Up close, Skelly was just as enigmatic as from afar. Her bones were in more severe disrepair than Josie imagined—cracked and the color of watered-down mustard. Her extended hand defied physics—nothing but air keeping the limb upright. The insides of her eye sockets were dusty and hollow, and even still Skelly's gaze was oppressive. Meeting Skelly's hand with her own, Josie fought the urge to recoil. Her bones were cold, disconnected. Josie's pinky slipped in between Skelly's knuckles when she squeezed. The entire ordeal was shiver-inducing and terrible, which was why she tripped on a vine in her rush to escape as soon as the deal was sealed.

In the time it took her to stand again, Skelly had disappeared.

"No, that's not creepy at all. Totally fine to just pop in and out of existence on a whim."

In cruder, more accurate phrasing, she was fucked.

Lucky for her, this was when Josie did her best work.

DAY FIVE

WHAT SHE EXPECTED to be a few hours of cleaning up her inbox and soothing neglected clients—a single day of unresponsive service, no matter the crisis, was unacceptable—morphed into an all-nighter apology tour. This left precious few hours to consider her task at hand—a story. Some kind of story. Something fresh, something new. Because this was a totally doable task Josie was prepared for and was not going to fail miserably at as soon as she opened her mouth.

She finished working at three in the morning, beat her espresso machine to death at five past three, then plopped herself at the kitchen table for approximately thirty minutes of sipping warmed-over espresso and blank wall staring. The only story that came to mind was Cinderella, quite possibly one of the most infamous tales of all in the western canon. She imagined the ways she could rearrange the familiar narrative, but every time she tried, it meandered its way back to the original. Or with Cinderella being a serial killer, which wasn't without its charms. She decided to keep that one in her pocket, just in case.

By four she realized that no amount of caffeine was going to keep her alert and decided to attack this again in the morning with some fresh eyes. Before shuffling off to bed—aka the couch—she typed an autoresponder on her email alerting her clients to expect delayed responses, then immediately deleted it. As she learned this evening, her client base was not in the least flexible—customer emergencies were immediate, somewhere between car explosions and a stolen identity, if on a scale. A delay of hours was often quantifiable in dollars, and both her clients and she herself had already taken a financial hit. Should she come out the other end of this in one piece, she needed to ensure she still had a viable business to rely on.

Her sleep was patchy and full of storms that cascaded into morning. Thunder rattled her windows, humming menacingly through her poorly insulated walls. She awoke to slanted rain pelting the glass, carried by a fierce wind whistling through the single pane. For a minute, she panicked that her dream had somehow followed her, manifesting itself in her reality like a virus. Then, she remembered she'd been dreaming and that her reality was much worse, and got up for her morning coffee.

Except it was noon. Dawn had slipped by under the clouds, and she was already four hours behind schedule.

Skelly had returned, upright in her throne, surrounded by a moat of mud and vines. Water shone silver along her form, a reflection of the pale afternoon sun. Rain sprayed off her bones, creating a mist that made her look even more ethereal than before.

She opened the door for Po, who'd been pawing the floor impatiently since she'd stepped into the kitchen. As he raced down the patio to his favorite rainy-day pee spot, she called out to Skelly.

"Good morning."

"*Good afternoon.*"

"I slept in today. For some reason, I was exhausted. I wonder why?"

"*I am very well rested.*"

"That's lovely for you."

"*Yes, it is.*"

Josie was suddenly aware of her empty hands and wished she'd made her coffee before going out, for the simple reason of occupying her fingers. And the caffeine.

"Do you even sleep?"

"*Sleep is for the living.*"

"So, you're dead?"

"*What do you consider dead?*"

"Being a skeleton is generally a good indicator."

"*Under normal circumstances, sure.*"

"But not now."

"*When was the last time a dead thing spoke to you?*"

"I see your point."

Skelly paused a moment before speaking again.

"*Have you thought of a story to tell?*"

"I've considered it."

"*It's Cinderella, isn't it?*"

Josie's hands stilled. "How did you know that?"

"*Your age, ethnicity, and current status indicate a certain upbringing that would be ripe with gentrified fairy tales, of which Cinderella is one of the most popular. It's a simple deduction.*"

"Or you've been spying on me."

"*I only go where I'm welcome.*"

"Can you clarify?"

"*Don't use your client speak here, Little Bird.*"

"I'm sure I have no idea what you're talking about," she said, trying to ignore the fact that the vines were now stirring at her feet.

"*For one, it doesn't make sense.*"

"Neither do clients."

"*You speak of them as if they are another species. Are you yourself not a client of someone else?*"

"Of course I am, and I can assure you I'm just as terrible. That's just how it goes."

"*Why do you say that?*"

Josie could feel herself slipping into an old argument, one she'd engaged in her own head on so many occasions that by the time she realized she was simply mimicking her own alter ego she was already deep in conversation. "I don't know, capitalism? The 'the customer is always right' mantra is steeped in it. When customers are satisfied enough to fork over cash for shit they don't need and don't value is all that matters. It means retailers and service providers engage in abusive relationships for a living and are compensated for the privilege."

"*Then why do it?*"

"Because there's a need. And a person has no idea how bad a job can get until they're already invested. Or they think their situation will be different than the rest. Or they have no other skills, at least not profitable ones. Or ... well, there are lots of reasons."

"*What is your reason?*"

Josie leveled a gaze at Skelly, so focused on her ribcage that her peripherals were fuzzy. "Probably all of them."

"*That's not true.*"

"How would you know if it was?"

"*Your posture, lack of eye contact, sudden rigidity, and pursed lips indicate that you are lying.*"

"So what if I am?"

"*Some might say that it would make an interesting story.*"

"Some might be wrong."

Po scratched at her calf, willing her to open the door so he could escape the rain.

"*How would you know if you've never told it?*" Before the statement had finished, a rush of vines congealed behind Josie, forming a chair much like Skelly's throne.

"I'm not sitting there."

"*It's only a chair.*"

"A sentient chair."

"*I think you'll find it quite comfortable.*"

Begrudgingly Josie sat, Po leaping into her lap. Vines twisted underneath her body, supporting her weight and frame perfectly. It was impressively comfortable and felt like another trap.

"*Have your clients ever asked about your business?*"

"Sure, and I repeat the same script every time. 'I saw a need that my skills could help fill. I wanted to help people, clients, and business owners alike, create a safe, professional line of communication. I wanted to provide the gift of rapport.' You know, a bunch of bullshit."

"*And they find this response acceptable?*"

"It isn't a question that demands a truthful answer. None of my clients care about my past, no more than I care about theirs. This is a transaction. They simply want to make sure I know how to speak a transactional language."

The rain picked up, pounding like rocks on her roof. "It's getting nasty out here."

"*You don't like the rain?*"

"I didn't say that." In fact, she loved the rain. The thicker the storm, the better. She liked storms loud and vicious, wind ripping shingles into another time zone. They weren't very frequent in the desert where she lived, even during monsoon season, which usually brought excessive dust storms and little else, coating everything in its path with a fine mist of dust that never seemed to come clean. Storms like this one, the kind that lent itself to myths of vengeful gods tearing the earth in two, were as rare as they were powerful.

"*There is a reason so many stories begin with storms.*"

"Yes, lots of cliché dark and stormy nights."

"*It's only cliché if you have a bad story.*"

"What is a bad story, by your standards?"

"*A bad story is a story told simply to hear oneself speak.*"

"I dare say you do a lot of that yourself, Skelly."

"Which is why I'm desperate to hear something new."

"Which is why I'm mystified that you arrived here instead of literally anywhere else."

"Oh, Little Bird, you are terribly dense."

Josie's interest in this conversation was waning. "Three days, was it?"

"Giving up so soon?"

"I'm not going to sit here just to be insulted. I could easily go inside and at least get paid for it."

"That would make it more suitable?"

"Money? Yeah."

"Then I will pay you."

"You'll pay me? With what?"

"Money, whichever form you choose."

"And where exactly are you going to get money?"

"That is the least of my restrictions, Little Bird. So, if it is money you seek, money I shall provide."

"Fine then, I want a gold bar."

There was another short pause. Josie was getting the feeling this indicated annoyance on Skelly's part.

"I am reminded of a story if you'd care to hear it."

"Do I have a choice?"

"Of course."

Josie expected Skelly to say no, so it perked her curiosity when she didn't. Despite her reservations, she was anxious to see what Skelly would say. "Don't touch me this time."

Skelly didn't acknowledge this demand, which was slightly worrying.

"This is a story of the people of thunder."

Vines lurched from the ground, water rolling from their forms in small waterfalls as they collected around the base of Skelly's throne.

"It is said that the people who speak in thunder live under our feet. They are a demure people, composed mostly of sulfur and rock. One might assume they don't speak at all, let alone with such a robust timbre, yet whenever you hear the sky begin to split apart, rest assured it is not the Gods of the sky, but the people of the earth itself calling to one from their dense, dark homes."

Vines jutted upward from their collection near Skelly's throne, looming over her head like a crown of clouds. The ground beneath her writhed in vines, sloshing rainwater at Josie's feet with ominous prophecy.

"They are the cleverest of people if you ask me. Thunder carries such a rumbling, ominous tone that most others hear only a warning and nothing more. The people of thunder could be chatting about their morning coffee, and not only would the rest of us bolt for shelter, but we'd also look up to the sky as we fled. Their method of misdirection is unparalleled."

Vines thickened in their cloud-shaped form before suddenly jutting toward the ground. Josie lifted her legs as they mapped their way across her yard, forming what appeared to her like a map of subway tunnels. Jagged hubs formed in between the tunnels, which Josie could only assume were meant to represent the thunder people.

"Those with wisdom and patience enough to deduce the nuance of their language can expect to be treated to some of the most skillful orators of our time, or any time. Yet, we refuse. We hear warnings and peril, the beauty lost against the thickness of our own skulls."

Josie cradled herself in her arms. The storm was aggressively pooling mud pockets in her yard, and the vines sloshing within them making sucking and slurping noises. The urge to flee into the house was unbearable.

"Perhaps that's the point," Josie said.

"Why do you think so?"

"Not every cry begs a response. Some people just need to scream."

"And why are they screaming?"

Josie couldn't decipher if it was from the storm in her yard or the storm of the story, but reflections of lightning bounced from vine to vine, appearing to her like some form of ancient Morse code.

"Who am I to say?"

"Indeed."

"Why are you telling me this?" She hated the feel of the vines at her back. Their unnatural shifting sent wild chills throughout her body. They felt like snakes, or bugs, or both.

"Oh, I am no better than your average, drunken bard. It is what I do."

"What is that supposed to mean?"

Water danced off Skelly's bones with ominous intent.

"I meant nothing by it."

"Did you call me a drunk?"

"No, but aren't you?"

Josie may as well have zipped herself into a body bag. Just like that, she was dead inside. The heavy lump she'd been carrying in her throat dissolved into the rest of her body, numbing her from head to toe. Po jumped from her lap. He was shivering and whimpering from inattention, desperate to get back inside the house and away from the cold and the wet and the vines and Skelly. Or maybe that was Josie. Either way, she rose from her seat and went inside without another word.

She grabbed a bottle of vodka, figuring that if everyone called her a drunk, she may not pretend otherwise anymore. It was time to drink. And drink and drink.

The day grew as dark as Josie's mood, a heaviness pulling down the shades of civility. A disharmonious chord vibrated throughout her body as she slammed into her vodka with vigor. Skelly didn't know anything. If she did, she wouldn't be haunting Josie's pathetic yard in search of pathetic stories told by a pathetic, lonely drunk. Skelly should know—she had to know—why Josie was crafted this way. It wasn't by accident, but design. Josie's design. The only thing she'd ever made that was just for her, by her, to suit her.

This little life was hers, and now this Skelly drops in and wants a piece of it. Josie was miffed as hell at the stupidity of their agreement. It reeked of so many pasts she thought she'd finally discarded, of silenced ghosts claiming new voices after Josie had shut them out. Somehow, those old regrets always found a way home.

Po trailed her step for step as he did every time she leaned hard into drinking like she couldn't be trusted to brush her teeth or take a shit on her own accord. Usually, by then, she was so hammered the insult of his attention became endearing, and it wasn't uncommon to find them both curled on the bathroom floor by the night's end. This was the direction they were heading before a knock sounded throughout the house. More like a pounding. Josie didn't even hear anything at first what with the storm raging mercilessly outside and her own thoughts being so loud.

She looked down at her hands, setting the vodka on the couch and thinking she ought to wash them. Spilled liquor slicked her skin, making her fingers stick together. Not that washing her hands would lend her any more credibility as a well-adjusted, normal adult, but still she felt compelled to clean herself before answering the door to whoever kept knocking. Then, her drunk ass started reminiscing about hand soap, and the urge faded.

"You know what, Po? I can't smell that soap anymore. You know the soap I'm talking about. The hospital soap. It all has that same industrial smell, totally stripped of the frill of refill hand soaps. There's no lilac in this soap. No cute clownfish on the plastic jug. It's soap with a purpose and it smells like astringent shit. The grocery store uses that soap. That's why I can't go back. You remember that day, right? The day I came home from the store three hours after I was supposed to be home. The day security had to assist me to my car, threatening to call the cops. I kept telling them about the soap, that it triggered something, and they kept calling me ma'am in a way that meant they were done listening to me. I don't go to that store anymore because of the soap. I'd rather smell my own shit than that soap. I'd rather get typhus or whatever disease you get when you don't wash your hands than smell that soap again, Po. It smells like the hospital where dad died, and I hate that smell. You get it. You're a good boy."

She was still riding her soapbox when the pounding sounded again, and she remembered why she was thinking of soap to begin with.

Whoever was on the other side was determined not to leave. She had no choice but to open the door. "What?"

Sue again. Annoying neighbor Sue. Completely unbothered by Josie's aloofness Sue. Porcelain face unwilling to flinch Sue. Josie wasn't even sure what time it was, therefore couldn't properly place the meaning behind Sue's visit. Was it Saturday? She was supposed to meet her Saturday.

"It's Friday," Josie said, without further explanation.

Inclement weather whipped like a dark curtain behind Sue's sturdy back. "You have a problem," she said.

No shit, Sue. No fucking shit. Josie gripped the edge of her door for stability, hoping her swagger wouldn't show.

"Which problem are you referring to exactly?"

Sue cocked her head in a way suggesting she'd made a grave miscalculation, then sucked on her teeth. "I think you should come look."

"Look, Sue. I'm a little busy right now. I'm pretty sure I'm supposed to be working or something. I don't know. I just know that I'm busy. You can save me a bunch of time by just telling me what you want instead of dragging me into the rain to see."

It was then that porcelain Sue's visage wrinkled a little bit, and though Josie might have been drunk, she was certain she saw explicit intent behind her response. "I fear you have a *vine* problem."

Ever the consummate professional, Josie spat back, "No, I don't." This, she hoped, would solve the issue as matter-of-factly as it was spoken.

And to her drunken surprise, it did not.

"So, the plants crawling over the top of your house are par for the course then?"

Her statement didn't register in the slightest. "Absolutely."

"You're very drunk."

"Yes, very." The syllables stressed into a slur. She was quite superbly, stupidly drunk. The conversation was also rapidly boring her. Vomiting was imminent.

Sue fiddled inside her fanny pack before shoving something pungent underneath Josie's nose. The putrid scent immediately stalled her rambling. To swat it away, she stumbled through the threshold of the door and into the rain.

The water was painful, shocking her as near to sobriety was possible. "What the fuck was that?"

Sue lurched toward her with urgency. "You need to deal with this." Hefting Josie by the arm, she directed her toward the front of her house.

She might have vomited right then if not for Sue's steady grip. Shit.

Cagey tendrils of green curled over the peak of her roof. From this distance, a person might confuse them as a trick of the brain, a storm mirage, shadows, and light reflecting in obtuse ways.

But Josie knew what they were. So did her neighbor.

Sue leaned into her; voice hushed yet still commanding. "Tell them to get down."

"Tell *what* to get down?"

"Those." Sue pointed, casual as could be, to the mounting botanical catastrophe oozing from her roof.

A slurry of questions begged for answers—or more accurately, every conceivable question a person could fathom when presented with such a situation. So bogged by their urgency, Josie simply said nothing for what seemed like minutes, glaring with a sharpness at Sue until a conglomerate of a question finally put itself together. "Who are you?"

After all that slow-moving work, all Sue could respond with was, "A concerned neighbor." Followed quickly by another command. "They're listening to you. Tell them to get down."

"I can't tell them to do anything. They're magic or some shit. They do whatever the hell they want."

"They most assuredly do *not*. Now, get control of yourself and tell them to get down."

The vines were actively slithering now, inching toward the two women with undeniable intent. Sue squared up, stepping between Josie and the house. "You are not a helpless babe. Make your command and they will listen."

Sue placed a hand on Josie's shoulder, which was the wrong move. Wet and drunk and stomach knotted in one too many ways, Josie's personality skipped toward annoyance with a swiftness. "Leave me the hell alone," she said.

"Nothing would delight me more," she said, posture at odds with her mouth. A passerby might confuse them for lovers the way Sue leaned into her.

Josie was ill-equipped for this. Annoyance evolved into something far more sinister and violent. She didn't just want Sue to leave her alone, she wanted to flail and kick until Sue had no choice but to give Josie a wide berth.

She didn't just want Sue to go away, she wanted everything and everyone to go away. Her skin itched with closeness, an invasive swarm of insects tickling her body with their too-many legs. A scream churned through her. She had to get away. She wanted them to go away.

Sue. The vines. Skelly. All of them.

She wanted the rain to stop. She wanted to be dry. She wanted to move, get in her car, and peel out with Po in the passenger seat.

But where would she go?

This was her place, her home. They needed to go.

"Get off my property, god damn it. All of you. Get the fuck out of here."

If her words carried beyond her two hands she'd have been surprised. Wind whipped her short hair into her eyes, suddenly wild. Sue faced away from her, toward the house. Both women watched as the vines slunk away, presumably disappearing into Josie's yard once again.

She took zero satisfaction in her success. The churn was still there, though less a scream than concentrated stomach bile at this point. Josie heaved and vomited in the gravel while Sue patted her head with perfunctory effort.

"That's better, isn't it?"

Curled over and puking was how Sue left her, but not before reminding Josie of her obligations.

"I'll see you tomorrow for tea. Ten a.m. It appears we will have much to discuss."

DAY SIX

THE NIGHT PASSED in a haze, rattled by storms so intense that when she awoke on her kitchen floor to a beam of morning scorching her eyes, she thought she had died. Once evident that this was not the case, she made herself some coffee and tried to chase away the disappointment. Her coffee was bad, probably because she didn't bother cleaning out yesterday's old grounds. The morning was bad because of her hangover. Her clothes stuck stiff to her skin and her lips were glued to the tile by a dried pool of drool.

Po was nowhere in sight, but his anxious tossing and turning from under the throw blanket on the couch eased her worry. She must have been in rougher shape than she imagined for him to be avoiding her like this. Calling his name made the rustling stop for a moment, but after a few seconds, it was evident Po was still quite chuffed. He refused to move.

"We'll see how committed you are once I get the milk bones out."

Besides, there were many more pressing issues at hand today, such as whether the events she thought happened last night had really happened, and if they did, happened the way she sorta kinda remembered. The fact that she couldn't quite tack down the truth made her sicker than the booze, the uncertainty dragging back a host of bad memories. At least, she didn't have an angry husband to contend with anymore. Stuart wasn't nearly as pliable with treats as Po was, so there was that.

There was, unfortunately, the new issue of Sue and what Sue

did or did not know. And Skelly, who was conspicuously missing in action. The vines themselves were tangled in a lump on her patio. For some reason, she anthropomorphized them to be sulking like a struck dog, which made her feel terrible. Because of course, she was the type to feel guilty for yelling at a plant. Of course, this is a thing she would feel.

This same guilty feeling was what had chipped away at her marriage, and even though Stuart had been free of her for two years now, Josie could still feel his sting. The argument played out in her head as if he was sitting across from her, hands folded over his mouth the way he did when trying to siphon his pain into a cogent conversation.

Do you remember what you did last night?
I did a lot of things.
Like?
Tell me what you want me to apologize for and I'll apologize.
Then why bother, Josie?
I'm not sure, Stuart. You started the conversation.

The memory carried with it a mélange of every flavor remorse imaginable, a veritable Baskins Robbins thirty-one flavors of shame. Most of the time she had acted like an ass and probably needed to be accountable. But all the time, Stuart had fancied himself the executor of her accountability—how it would be acknowledged and atoned all flowed through him. It was this act that she could never reconcile, and consequently her own actions as well. They had both slipped into their individual version of toxicity and by the end, they were so reactionary to the other's existence that an out-of-place sneeze would rocket them toward war.

This was when her mother texted her.

Do you have your dad's piggy bank?

This wasn't a question. Ma knew exactly where all of Dad's

stuff was.

I can't recall dad ever owning a piggy bank

It looked like a baseball helmet

That was a piggy bank?

It was full of pennies. That's why it was so heavy

Oh

Do you have it?

IDK there's a lot of stuff

Will you look?

Why

I was just thinking about it

There are so many boxes

I want to put it on the boat

Do you even have room for more of his stuff?

One piggy bank won't sink the boat

I'll let you know if I find it

Dad would have wanted it here

Josie dropped her phone and looked over her shoulder, half expecting her mother's poltergeist to be haunting her hallway in the accusatory way only her mother could manage. Josie didn't hate her mother, or even dislike her really—much to the credit of her dad—but they were never close. Josie considered them more like two ships passing in the night rather than mother and daughter. The irony wasn't lost on her that her mother now lived exclusively on a boat.

Josie glanced at the cabinet over the fridge. Her knickknack cabinet. The place where odd-sized platters and strange cutlery with indefinable uses were kept. This was where things that had no place lived. A place of lost things she referenced so infrequently because she needed to climb on her countertops to reach them. This was where she currently hid the piggy bank her mother wanted.

She'd deal with that later. Josie texted her mother back that she'd look for it, despite having zero intention of following up.

Sipping her coffee, she did everything possible to occupy her mind and not throw it up again. Turns out her thirty-something body wasn't nearly as adaptable as a twenty-something to an all-night bender anymore—the spirit of fun and carefree wildness now missing from such an occasion. Turned out panic drinking wasn't healthy for a person. Weird.

There were many things she needed to get done today, most importantly, her clients. Her decision to not engage an autoreply was regrettable. She probably lost far more business due to her neglect than she would have if she'd just set up the goddamn autoreply, but she needed to sober up a bit more before attempting to navigate that field of landmines. No one was expecting anything from her on a Saturday anyway. May as well take her time.

Then, there was tea with Sue some time today. Wait—what time was it?

Her oven clock beamed a discouraging time at her. Nine-thirty in the morning. Ten was tea—she thought. That left a paltry thirty minutes to sober up, stop feeling like death, feed Po, clean the vomit off the toilet, dress, and make her way over to Sue's house in one piece. A sense of dread cooled the effect of the coffee, mainly because she couldn't yet piece together what had really happened last night. While part of her wished the entire scenario away, another part was more curious than she'd ever been about anything. The steady hopelessness of Skelly's arrival was now punctuated with a bit of agency. If Josie hadn't been hallucinating, then Sue *knew* something.

If Josie was wrong, however, then there was a sincere chance Sue would have her committed by the end of tea. She had to be smart about this.

With one more peek into the yard to verify Skelly's absence, Josie set about beautifying herself for the encounter. Feeding Po was simple—he'd already managed to chew through the bag of food and eat his fill, hence his lack of hustle this morning. The bathroom was in better sorts than she figured. Must have completed most of the vomiting outside, which too was conveniently washed clean by the rain. Disinfectant wipes in hand, she scrubbed the dried spots on the porcelain and worked on her conversation starters. It benefitted her to have more than one to choose from.

That was some storm last night. Never seen anything like it, have you?

You didn't get too wet, did you?

Sorry, I'm feeling a bit under the weather this morning on account of last night.

I was curious, Sue, about your opinions of sentient vines?

Might I ask what the fuck it is you know about magic plants? Additionally, I may have hallucinated some wild shit if you don't mind indulging me.

Have you ever spoken to a skeleton and had it speak back?

Certainly, none of these would come across as insane. Meanwhile, her body and hair looked as if it had been whipped through a blender full of rocks. She was off to a great start here.

Somehow, Josie managed to put herself through the motions enough to get out the door. Po observed her from his perch atop the back of the couch, cautious of her boldness. Allowing herself a moment of smug satisfaction at his expense, she gave him a little wave as she slipped from the house and immediately tripped on a rock placed on her doorstep. Po didn't even bother to leave the couch, just stuffed his snout through the curtain and watched as she picked herself up, plucking bits of embedded gravel from her palms.

"What is a rock doing there?" She made sure to exclaim this forcefully, reiterating to any observing neighbors the innocence of the fall, which was not at all related to her drunken escapades. Dusting herself off, she went to move the rock aside and stopped in her tracks—it wasn't a rock, it was gold. A gold bar to be exact. The shadows of the porch concealed the rich gleam, but from this direction, it glittered like gold. Because it *was* gold.

All doubts of authenticity were absolved the moment she touched it. Even for gold, which she supposed was heavy, the bar was deceptively dense. It probably weighed about twenty pounds or more, which made its arrival on her porch even more suspicious and confusing.

Suspicious and confusing, until she remembered her conversation with Skelly the previous day. Something about being paid. Something about gold bars.

Still, where did Skelly find this thing? Josie wondered what kind of warrants were out in her name as she hid the bar in an empty pot on the porch. Leave it to Skelly to find a way to turn a simple business transaction into a bank robbery. Maybe she could use the money to buy Sue's silence when Josie went on the lam.

Sue opened the door just as Josie approached as if she'd been watching through the peephole.

"I wasn't sure you'd make it."

"Surprise," Josie said with a little too much enthusiasm.

"Well, come in. You probably want to sit."

Sue ushered her inside her home, keeping a close yet impersonal distance behind her. The house was as mismanaged and chaotic as Josie had imagined—boxes spilled into other boxes, tossed sloppily in the corner. By appearances, there hadn't been any attempt to unpack. The walls were bare and dirty, the dust on the floors puffing under Josie's steps. If she ventured a guess, she'd say no one had bothered living inside this house at all. None of this seemed to fluster Sue, who made none of the customary attempts to excuse the conditions of her home. This was good for Josie, who had precious little energy to think of something nice to say.

Ah, yes, these dirt eddies are simply charming. How rustic of you to never use a broom.

Neither statement was even remotely fair considering the state of her own home, but the sarcasm was tough to meter at times. Her natural snark ended up being irrelevant, however, the moment Josie stepped through the threshold into Sue's backyard.

It was paradise.

Josie was at a loss for words. The house was located on a bend of the cul-de-sac and therefore had an oblong shape. The state of the front yard and house led Josie to believe the back was in similar disrepair. Instead, she found herself transported to a garden fit for royalty. Vines weaved through white trellises lining the discolored fence. The grass was a deep, healthy green, not a yellowing patch in sight. Wildflowers and roses sprouted from planters running the edge of the patio, and in the center of the yard stood two newly planted citrus saplings.

The patio itself housed a table already set for two, a teapot and carafe of coffee sandwiched by two opened packages of cookies. Sue motioned to a seat, flipping over the upside-down mug before taking a seat opposite her.

"I spend most of my time out here," she said.

"I can see that."

"The trellises were already here, just had to paint them. I planted those orange trees yesterday." Sue indicated toward the refreshments on the table.

"Tea, for now, is fine."

After pouring them each some tea, she leaned back in her chair and nibbled on a shortbread cookie. "I'm a bit of a green thumb, as you can see."

"That so?" Josie sipped the tea, some sort of herbal spicy something she couldn't quite put her finger on, but pleasant, nonetheless.

Sue continued. "Something we have in common, don't you think?"

"No. Not really."

"Not much of a gardener?"

"I wouldn't say so." She wasn't exactly clear what they were talking about, so Josie left it at that.

"Well." Sue sipped her tea. "Regardless of your interests, I'd say you have quite a way with plants."

"That's funny," she said.

"Why do you say that?"

"Just ..." Why did she say that? "I think this is the first time anyone has described me as having a way with plants."

"A contentious relationship?" Sue raised a brow while finishing her cookie.

Josie wasn't sure which relationship she was referring to, but the answer to that question was still a unilateral yes. "How long have you, you know, liked plants?"

Her inner eloquence screamed on loop at how stupid she sounded, but Sue cocked her head to one side as if this was a question she'd never yet encountered.

"Years."

"Years?"

"Since I was about your age."

Josie fiddled with how to proceed. Were they talking about

the vines or just gardening in general? "And what would you say prompted your interest? In plants, I mean."

"I guess I'd say I ran across a very weird one once. You know how it goes."

"I know what you mean." She thought she did, at least. "Did you ever find out what it was?"

In impersonating a normal human, Josie realized she'd been sitting since the start of the conversation with the mug frozen to her face. She set it down with more force than intended, then crossed her arms and pretended it was all part of the plan in asserting herself as the neighborhood eccentric.

"I never did figure it out," Sue said. "Not entirely."

"Oh."

Before Josie could wallow in what this may mean for her own situation, Sue pointed over Josie's shoulder before freeing another cookie from the pack.

Dread drowned out all sound. Josie knew without looking what Sue was indicating. All this talk about plants and weirdness had Josie hyper-focused on the vines in her yard, and like all irritating things in her life, the more she focused on them, the more they came to play. Her mother was a prime example.

"They're there, aren't they?" she asked, not wanting to face them.

"Yes, they are."

"Vines."

"Yes, your vines are here."

"They are not my vines," Josie said, astounded by Sue's cavalier reaction.

"Of course not. They don't belong to anyone, but it does seem they've taken a particular interest in you." She slurped her tea before ominously adding, "For some reason."

Josie tightened her arm cross. "Care to enlighten me?"

"About what?"

"About what you know of those things? These are the weird plants you were talking about before, yes?"

"These are different, but I suspect they come from the same family."

"Why do you say that?"

Sue rose from the table. "Well, for one, mine always flower." Waving her hand over the nearest rosebud, the petals instantly drew into a tight coil, reopening again as she returned to her seat.

Transfixed, Josie felt the entire world slow to a crawl as the petals unfurled to the former grandeur. "How did you do that?"

"I asked them."

"Them?"

"The plants."

Josie's chest hammered with excitement. Or was it anxiety? It didn't matter because Sue *knew*. She was there last night. She'd known what to do. She saw them, too. "What about … the others?"

If talking to plants wasn't a thing that fazed Sue, the prospect of Skelly's existence wouldn't be much of a stretch, but for some reason, Josie couldn't bring herself to acknowledge it out loud.

"What others?"

A momentary panic struck, and Josie considered abandoning the conversation for safer waters, but then again, fuck it. When would an opportunity like this present itself again?

"You've only ever seen the plants?"

"You mean to tell me that you've seen more?"

"I don't know. I'm not sure. Maybe? What kind of cookies are those?"

Nudging the package, Sue said, "They're shortbread cookies. My favorite. Try some, and then tell me what you have seen."

Josie obliged, stroking the edge of the cookie with her

thumb before taking a bite. "Why don't you tell me what *you* have seen?"

"Something tells me your story will be better."

"Why exactly? Wait, what brand are these cookies? They're fucking delicious."

"Generic grocery store brand from up the street, but you have to get them in the southwest chains. The supplier must be different in other areas because they just aren't the same. Don't crumble as well. Less buttery."

Josie hummed with approval. Could be from the hangover or maybe just a nice distraction from a tough conversation, but these cookies really were top-notch. She'd have to remember to add them to her next grocery delivery.

"Now, as for your predicament. You owe me no explanation and I won't push you for one, but what I can say is that I have never seen plants move the way your vines move. In all my years, in all my experience with such … things, never have they been so animated. Now, there could be a multitude of reasons why. I have my theories, but I won't bore you with them, principally because I'm not sure how much you know and therefore how much to explain. But, if you'll indulge me, might I offer some advice?"

It was bizarre to be asked such a thing. She wasn't used to such a courtesy, especially considering her line of work. "Sure."

"You need to figure out what they want—what about you attracts them. These vines are aggressive. I don't doubt they would turn you to bone if given the chance."

Josie froze, crumbs trickling down her lip. "What did you say?"

The expression on Sue's face wavered so imperceptibly Josie almost missed it. "I said they will turn you to bone."

Trying to ignore the slithering noise behind her as well as to add emphasis to what she was about to say, Josie leaned over the table. "You have met her, haven't you?"

Meeting her lean, Sue nodded.

"Skelly?"

"Oh, is that the name she gave you?"

Josie scowled. "Did she tell you a different name?"

Sue bit a cookie. "She gave me none at all, though to be fair, I never asked."

"We are talking about Skelly, right? The skeleton. The one that talks and is currently roosting like a hen in my backyard."

To this Sue chuckled, winding her fingers around the handle of her mug without taking a sip. "A name was never needed. She was just there. There was never any confusion as to who I was talking to as the words just came. And she heard. And she spoke back."

It was a deep relief to hear this, and as Josie fiddled with her cookie, she felt the knot in her chest slowly, carefully unspool. "How did you make her stop?"

"Pardon?"

"How did you make her go away?"

"Who said she ever did?"

Whatever relief her insides were granted immediately reversed, leaving her tenser than before. Perhaps the scientists she'd eventually will her cadaver to would discover how a person could attain such mythic levels of anxiety. Until then, she'd be here sipping tea and collapsing like a black hole.

"I knew I shouldn't have made that deal. Fuck."

Now it was Sue's turn to be astonished. "What deal?"

"The deal? Wait, did I fuck up? Like I know I did, that's not up for debate, but did I *really* fuck up?"

"What exactly did you agree to?"

Perhaps she hadn't been wise to hand out all this background information so freely. What did she even know about Sue, aside from her excellent taste in cookies and poor taste in fanny packs? "I'm not exactly sure."

"That's encouraging."

"Well, excuse me if, in a moment of desperation, I made an ill-advised handshake deal with an inhuman creature."

"You shook her hand?"

"I was under duress!"

"That's irrelevant."

"I disagree." Josie reached for another cookie, taking three in one hand and daring Sue to say anything about it. "Besides, why don't you just ask her yourself? You said she never left."

"It doesn't work like that. I can't just call her on the phone."

"Who said anything about a phone? She's literally right on the other side of this fence. She's probably listening to our conversation as we speak."

The women paused, both having not considered this until spoken aloud. Josie had avoided a backward glance because of the vines, but now she couldn't get the idea of Skelly with her bald skull pressed against the concrete blocks, straining to catch the newest gossip. Not that Skelly, with all her infinite wisdom and power, would need to do such a thing—although she might, if only to be a condescending ass.

Then again, Josie had a sense—maybe the same thing Sue mentioned—of when Skelly was present and ready to engage. The sensation was soundless and motionless but pulled on Josie's core like a magnet. She didn't feel it now. Still, she looked.

Vines curled over the lip of the fence, feeling their way into Sue's yard as if blind and stopping inches from Josie's feet. She yanked her body away from them, squishing both legs onto the small patio chair. "I don't think Skelly's there."

Sue drummed her fingers against the table. "She isn't."

"Where does she go? And how do I get her to stay there?"

"The answer to both questions is 'I don't know.'"

"Great."

"This is out of character," Sue said, staring into the distance.

"What's out of character?"

"What did she feel like?"

Josie did not like the suggestion that Skelly's bizarre behavior was even more out of character than already suspected.

"She felt like bone. Cold and dusty and old. She felt like a dusty corpse."

"Did she say anything else?"

"She said a lot of things, but I'd like to know exactly what you consider out of character. Her entire existence is out of character if you ask me."

Sue waved away her question, a sour expression twisting her lips. "The whole thing. A deal, allowing you to touch her. You, of all people."

"What is that supposed to mean?"

"It means exactly what you think. Who are you, really?"

The conversation was speeding into oncoming traffic. "I am no one. Just a sad, single lady living with her dog. I've done nothing. I've been nothing. I have nothing on my horizon, so if you're trying to insinuate that Skelly getting all chummy with me is because of some mystical heritage on my part, I'm here to tell you that is absurd."

"I'm thinking out loud," Sue said, shoulders straightening with every word. "And besides, you completely misinterpreted what I meant."

"I assume you don't need me to stick around then if you aren't even speaking to me directly." Josie rose to leave, but Sue snatched at her wrist, seating her again with the intensity of her glare.

"I'm afraid I don't have the answers you really want. I don't know why she chose you—or why she chooses anybody for that matter. I don't know what she wants from you. She seems to want different things from different people. I don't know why the vines are so attracted to you or why they are so … lively."

She tried to cut Sue's speech short with a snotty dismissal, but the woman held up a commanding hand that stayed her mouth.

"But here is what I do know—she has been silent for quite a while. I haven't spoken to her in years before now. And she has never, in my knowledge and experience, allowed anyone to touch her."

"Not like I wanted to, she basically made me."

"To seal the deal."

Josie nodded.

"I have no idea what she is up to."

Josie was instantly aware of the chair in which she sat—every rod, rim, and pattern—as if branding itself into her skin. The desire to get out of dodge was immediate. Sue's befuddlement wasn't an act, which was upsetting.

"She asked me to tell her a story. That was the deal. I had three days to come up with a story she'd never heard before. How do I come up with a story a thing like her has never heard?"

Dragging her finger over the rim of her mug, Sue lifted her cup for a drink but changed her mind. "A story?"

"I keep thinking about fairy tales, but there's a reason I can recall those without working too hard. They're part of the narrative already, implanted in the collective soul or something. I don't know, I'm sounding stupid right now. I'm just at a loss. I went to talk to her yesterday and things went poorly. I think she can read minds."

Sue scoffed, but not in an offensive way. "I don't think she can, actually. I do think she's lived long enough to understand the human condition in a way neither you nor I could ever fathom."

"Which makes our deal all the more insulting. What the fuck does she expect to learn from me?"

"Perhaps that's why she asked."

"What do you mean?"

"Maybe this has less to do with you than you think."

"Like she's having some sort of existential crisis or something?"

Sue settled back in her seat, plucking another cookie from the package. "I wouldn't go that far. Besides, if she were to have an existential crisis, as you put it, I'd expect it to have happened a millennia ago. Her behavior is odd, though. Something has prompted this, and I'm not entirely sure it has much to do with you."

"Well, that isn't exactly encouraging, Sue. Because I was fine before she and the vines rolled up. Just living my little life. It took forever to carve out a little piece of sanity for myself after the divorce and my dad and all that, and just when I get settled, Skelly shows up like a fucking firecracker in my oven. I didn't ask for her interference and I don't want it now that it's here. I just want her to leave me alone."

Josie kept careful watch of the flaring expressions on Sue's face—all of them so minute another person might have missed them. Her twist of the lips could be mistaken for a twitch, a flash of her brown eyes only a brief reflection of the afternoon sun, and her slow, creeping smile that was gone as soon as it started. If not for Josie's developed skill of reading faces in the absence of spoken words—reference; her marriage, her mother, et cetera—she might not have caught the amusement. But she did, which made what Sue said next even more unsettling.

"That's where you are wrong, Josie dear. For your Skelly, as she's named herself, never goes where she's not invited."

Josie hovered over her knees. Her body was a tight ball of bad decisions. After tea and cookies with Sue, she'd returned home and wretched everything she'd just consumed, still purging the previous night from her body. Afterward, everything shut down—her arms, legs, fingers, and brain, each powering down like a busted robot until nothing but the very basics operated on their own accord. Sleep crashed into her, and when she finally awoke the house was visible only from the glow of her phone.

Her first thought went to Po, who she discovered tucked under her right knee, hot with sleep and snoring. He stretched his paws and whined as she righted herself, both fighting off the delirium of an epic nap.

The previous night and tea and Sue and vines all seemed like a bad dream. It took her more than a few minutes to sort herself out, flipping on lights as she tripped through the house toward the kitchen. Every fiber of her body needed water. She didn't even bother with the Brita filter pitcher in the fridge and used the nearest cup to funnel water down her throat, most of which landed on the front of her shirt. Her hair and pants were sticky with sweat. She leaned against the counter and tried to piece out the past few days in her head.

Had she fallen asleep so hard that she had one of those out-of-body experiences? A lucid dream? She'd heard of them lasting days, or what seemed like days to the dreamer. Could that be what had happened to her?

There was a simple way to answer her question—just peek outside—but her feet rooted themselves to the tile, terrified on behalf of her sanity to dispel the easy notion that none of the past few days had been real. The split-second comfort of slipping back into her old life was intoxicating.

Then she remembered the gold. A quick answer and she could avoid the yard altogether. Trotting at her heels was Po, chittering nervously. How long had she been asleep? He was probably hungry.

The front door was unlocked and ajar, which was a fun discovery after a blackout nap, but she didn't have the energy to worry about an intruder on the premises. Po's nervous but silent demeanor meant if someone had tried to enter her home, they were long gone by now. Po would never let a stranger root around the living room without a good shouting.

Flinging the door open, her eyes fell to the pot where she'd stashed the gold bar. If gone, it could mean someone had stolen it, or she'd lost it or moved it in her sleep. Or that the gold had been a figment of her imagination.

As she leaned over the pot a glittery, golden brick winked back at her.

Josie didn't bother closing the door as she wobbled to the back of the house, tossing hand-tacked sheets over Po as she ripped her makeshift drapes from the wall. She wasn't even sure what to expect—perhaps Skelly leering at her just on the other side of the glass, or vines writhing like ooze across the patio floor. What she saw instead was darkness. Disoriented and awaiting the bleary moonlight to filter through the window she instead received darkness, but upon closer inspection, she realized why—vines. The shadows cast upon them from her kitchen light exposed all the nooks and crannies of their forms weaving in and out and in between one another and forming an impenetrable blockade.

Not even the door budged as she yanked on the handle as if they'd suctioned themselves to the glass. Nosing his way out of the clump of sheets, Po issued an irritated yelp before settling himself on his kitchen chair.

Lacking any better ideas, Josie pounded on the glass the same way she did when Po barked too much at the sound of a distant lawnmower. The vines, however, were less impressed with her frustration, which was to say they showed zero indication of moving at all.

She pounded again, this time with more force. "Get the fuck off my door," she said.

At her explicit command, they moved. Vines unknotted with intricate flurries, zipping away from the house and curling around Skelly's center throne. Atop the throne sat Skelly herself, glaring in Josie's immediate direction.

Despite the gold and the vines, Josie had still clung to some sort of hope that Skelly would be gone. Seeing her sent dread crashing to Josie's feet.

Skelly didn't speak as Josie slipped through the door, calming her jangled nerves by leaning against the wall. A wave of post-hangover nausea stilled her annoyance, afraid of what might come out if she opened her mouth.

"Feeling better?"

Josie simply stared at her. She was not better. If anything, she felt much, much worse.

"That was one hell of a bender, Little Bird. Something for the ages."

"The bards shall speak of it long after my passing, no doubt."

"Yes, we will."

"Oh, so you're a bard now?"

"I've already explained I am."

"That's not what Sue thinks." Though saying this did not fluster Skelly in the slightest.

"And what does our dear Sue think?"

Sue had no idea, just conjecture and theories. Her neighbor hadn't mentioned anything about what she thought Skelly might be, but at least they were talking now. Josie refused to let the opportunity go to waste.

"She seemed to think you were behaving strangely. Even for you."

Skelly seemed to consider this, or Josie intimated she might be considering this due to her lack of immediate retort.

"Strange to her does not equivocally mean strange."

"Is there a strangeness threshold I'm not aware of?"

"If there was, my threshold would be vastly different than yours."

"Did you appear to Sue the same way you have to me?"

"And how have I appeared to you?"

"A nuisance. A squatter." Even as she said this, Sue's castigation was in the back of her mind, looping over and over.

She never goes where she's not invited.

Josie wanted to ask Skelly more but knew if she did Skelly would only talk circles around her, replacing the answer with ten more questions.

"Why do you assume that?"

"Because all I want is for you to leave and you refuse." Nausea welled up again. She swallowed it down.

"And if that were truly the case, I would."

Having sat on the comment an entire two seconds, she said, "Sue said you never go anywhere you're not invited." Subtlety was never one of her strong suits.

"Sue is correct."

"Well, I didn't invite you here."

"Not politely, you didn't. In fact, I would say right now is a terribly inconvenient time for me to be tied up, but such is life."

"That wouldn't have something to do with the three-day time frame you gave me?"

"Maybe."

"What is going to happen at the end of the three days?"

"Why?"

"Because if I'm just going to die, I might as well go relax and watch TV or something, instead of being nauseous out here with you."

"Why don't you take a seat?"

Vines raced toward her, tangling into a cushion for Josie to sit. Apprehensive at first, her exhaustion soon overrode all other senses.

"*How about a quick little story?*"

"I'm tired of stories."

"*Impossible. Besides, I feel this one might be of particular interest to you.*"

This did not sound promising whatsoever. Not one little bit.

"*This is a simple story. A story of a father who would take his child out to sea. They would bounce over the waves in their small boat, never speaking to one another. Both said this was because the wind was too loud, the waves too mesmerizing, and still both wondered if it wasn't because neither had much to say.*

"*Every time they boarded their boat, the father would ask the daughter if she'd like to learn how to drive. Driving wasn't difficult and perfectly within the daughter's capabilities. A lesson or two and she would have mastered it. But her answer was always the same. What do you think it was?*"

The question did not register as Josie was certain she was midway through a minor stroke. She knew this story. It was her story.

How did Skelly know this story and why was she telling it? What was she doing, uprooting pieces of her that were never meant to be unearthed? Rage didn't course through her, but rather something else. Something emptying, a vacuum.

"*The answer was always no. Not out of spite or irritation or even laziness, rather out of comfort. Her place was a worn spot near the starboard side, cushion darkened by the many visits of her body. The father whizzed them over the waves, wholly in command. Each of them observers, those who knew them would say nothing slipped past them, but here on the ocean these two left their bodies, forgot about everything before and behind them, and floated. This was their passion, and it was never the same when a guest tagged along, as rarely as that happened. Most who invaded this bonded space never desired to return, acutely aware of the violation the moment the boat rocked against the docks upon boarding.*

"Until the father became ill. Fatigue. Pneumonia. Upper respiratory issues and recurrent sinus infections. The price of getting older, they thought. And they were right, however naïve of the cost. Disease soon anchored them to shore, suffocating them both more viciously than the cancer. The daughter decided to teach herself how to drive the boat. She took lessons in between doctor's visits and hospital stays. She hired a captain for a day. She traveled to the docks and washed the outside of the boat, became scuba certified, and dove beneath to scrub the barnacles off the hull. She replaced the brittle pieces corroded by salt, all the while assuring her father that one day they would return to the sea, and when they did, she promised to let him teach her to drive, refusing to steal the honor of passing his knowledge to her the way all of the most valuable knowledge is passed. He needn't know of her lessons, only marvel at her skill, at his gift of teaching. He might understand the truth, but that was irrelevant. They rarely spoke anyway."

Josie was unaware of her surroundings—oblivious to the agitated writhing of the vines. Her brain blacked out the present, starting a loop of bad memories. If she'd been aware of her surroundings in any fashion, she'd have noticed the strangle of vines surrounding Skelly's plant throne, seen them curl through the empty spaces between bones as she spoke. She'd have heard their soft shivering voices as they brushed against one another, consuming Skelly entirely until all that indicated her presence was her penetrating voice ringing in Josie's skull. Despite the vines winding through Skelly's mouth, it was Josie who couldn't speak. Her chest was a bomb threatening to blow, a panic attack within a panic attack within a panic attack—layers of them rooted so deeply that unearthing them might cause her skin to melt like a preserved body exposed to oxygen.

What she needed to do was scream, or cry, and drink. Or all three. Anything but freeze in place, yet her body refused. She was properly rooted to the ground, nowhere to go, nothing to blot out Skelly's words.

Skelly kept on, ambivalent.

"You can guess what happens next, can't you Little Bird? You know how these stories go because they aren't new. They are the oldest kind known to man, and the most potent of all, no matter the age. Perhaps that is why they persist, they endure. Because they are everything—a soul, a heart, humanity broken and raw. These are the stories that crack you open like a soft egg, don't they Little Bird? They touch the one thing all humans have in common, and they sting, no matter how far removed one might be from the characters."

"Why?" One word was all Josie could manage to say without throwing up.

"You know why."

Why are you telling me this? Why are you torturing me with it? Why are you here? Why do you know this? Why is it relevant? Why? Whywhywhywhy?

Skelly answered again, the edge evaporated slightly.

"You know why, Little Bird. I know you do. Why then, do you ignore the answer?"

A motion stirred inside her gut, something alien and sentient and always there. It felt like a snake. Or a vine, moving and awake. Josie calmed in an instant, not because the sensation was a comfort, but because, for once, she'd encountered something more terrifying than her memories.

"I have no idea what you're talking about," she said.

"Truly?"

But Josie was already thrashing the vines away and nearing the door. "I don't want to talk anymore."

"Curious, considering how little you speak already."

"Have a good night," she said, shutting the door on Skelly with calculated calm.

Josie hadn't dared to look behind her, but if she had, she'd have seen Skelly's bony forearm thrust itself free of its confines, vines falling limp at the base of her throne. If Josie had been paying attention, she might have noticed the greenness of the yard, no longer puckered with vines but flourishing with new growth that gleamed under the moon.

She might have seen the new way her small, unencumbered space had begun to thrive, or how the greens, new and less new, leaned ever so slightly in the direction of her house. To the door, more specifically. She might have sensed the tremor in the earth as she slammed the door, and the strange quality of moonlight gazing upon her back.

Instead, she locked the door, reattached the sheets to the wall, shut off the lights, and sat in the darkness until morning.

DAY SEVEN

THE NIGHT PASSED surprisingly quickly, or else she'd simply blacked out again. Whatever the reason, her mind was near empty of anything. The morning after a sleepless night usually brought a fresh bloom of anxiety over all the ways she had not slept and most certainly should have slept and how torturous this new day would be as a result. Her only thought on this morning was that she needed coffee, and lots of it, immediately.

Po maintained a cautious distance, eventually coming around at the rattle of his treat box. Even though he'd shredded his bag of food and likely scarfed down a week's worth of meals in a single evening, he couldn't resist the idea of a treat. Still, he didn't inhale it with his usual vigor, instead stealing away to the couch, nibbling on the edges of his snack while eyeing Josie with distaste.

That was okay. She was determined to get things under control. The past few days had spiraled so out of control she was surprised to find herself still functional. She was going to get on track again. Yes, she would.

She would.

Her first task was cleaning the house. The kitchen was a disaster—espresso grounds scattered all over the counter which attracted ants again, cabinet doors left gaping, and her floor was smudged to hell. After coaxing her coffeemaker into a quadruple shot espresso, she slammed her drink back in a gulp and got to work, starting immediately with the ants. She'd had this problem before. They weren't regular ants, just tiny black ones and they seemed infernally addicted to loose grounds in particular. Having rid herself of them a few times before, she knew she could again, but only with rigorous cleaning. If even a single speck of coffee was left unattended, the army would return en masse.

An indistinguishable amount of time passed in her vigor—organizing, cleaning, scrubbing, bleaching, sweeping, mopping, and laying out sticky pads on the windowsills in the hopes of trapping any lingering insects. By the time she'd finished cleaning her bathroom, the churn in her gut had morphed into a sharp ache. She was starving.

Po tottered into the kitchen, inserting himself on his usual chair. The dog was nothing if not predictable. So was she, which was why they got along so well.

For all the exploits of the week, she'd neglected her pantry. All she had to eat were some crackers and an old packet of ramen. She usually kept her food stores rather boring and sparse, but this was worse than normal. She went for her phone, ready to place an online grocery order, and only then realized her back pocket was empty.

"Where did I leave my phone, Po?" she asked. Her laptop centered her table, but no phone. She tried to not think of her clients as she searched further. There wasn't much she could do to mitigate the impending disaster anyway—what would she say to angry clients that would both pacify them and boost confidence in her reliability? She'd probably call it a personal emergency, but a person in her position could only claim that so many times. Customers didn't tolerate personal emergencies but usually kept quiet because rooted somewhere deep below their leathery, customer-is-king veneer lived the remaining vestiges of their humanity. Still, customers didn't like to be reminded that a person they used for a service was a human being existing outside the sphere of said service. This was one of the primary tenets of her customer service guide, one she tried to teach her own clients whilst they behaved just as terribly to her as their customers did to them. And round and round they went.

She eventually found her phone pinned between two couch cushions. The battery was dead, and once plugged in a slew of missed text messages flared across the screen. Her mother was prolific on this lovely Sunday morning.

Have you found the helmet?

I'm going to use it as a bookend

I know what starboard is now, because of all these books

Are you there?

Are you hungover?

When are you coming to the boat?

Text me when you get this

Then, as if her mother's incessant ramblings weren't enough, another more sinister text punctuated the lot.

Your mother says she can't reach you and wants me to check on you. Are you drunk?

And another—

I really wish you'd stop doing this. For everyone's sake

Ah, yes. For *everyone*. Everyone meaning him, Mr. Stuart Ex-Husband. The notion that he not only didn't want to be married to her but actively loathed being reminded of their union in general was the real kick in the teeth. Had it all been so bad?

Somehow, she was back in the kitchen, not remembering the exact moment she got there from the couch. Her phone buzzed from the other room as it remembered everything she had forgotten. Her eyes traveled to the top of the cabinets where she kept her many bottles of liquor, vodka mainly, each of the four surviving bottles perfectly lined. There wasn't any reason she kept them up there—she had no kids, no visitors, no one besides her and the dog that might ever lay eyes upon them, and still she placed them out of reach. Force of habit, perhaps. The top of the fridge was where her parents kept all the liquor growing up. It's where Stuart shoved the bottles so they were "out of the way" but he was hoping they were just inconveniently placed enough that she might give up trying to empty them down her throat.

She was probably an alcoholic, but she didn't like to think about that too much. Who wasn't, nowadays? She'd tried hard to limit herself, to be a responsible adult. A sensible adult and she'd been trying to do better. Only a few drinks per night instead of the blackout escapades from before. Well, just a few blackouts. Only one a week, maybe twice if she was in a good mood. But how long between benders was enough? How good did she have to be to erase all the bad? Was that even possible? She suspected Stuart didn't think so, and she hated him for it. Or maybe hated herself for still caring what he thought of her.

If a change of mind wasn't possible if all anyone thought of her was that she was an unhinged drunk, what was the point of sobriety anyway?

The point was to prove she could. Not to them, but to her. Because if she couldn't control herself then it meant he'd always been right about her. She was broken and he just didn't have the patience for her problems. No tolerance for expression outside of his own metric of productive expression. Life had to serve a purpose, had to be moving forward—and forward only—when all she wanted was to place her soul in his hands and let it exist. Maybe let someone else take care of it for a while. At least, she knew it would be safe.

But maybe that was just too much to ask of another person.

She placed the bottles on the counter, unscrewed each of them, then ceremoniously poured each of their contents down the drain. On the last of them, she hesitated. Skelly had given her three days, insinuating something was about to go sideways in a major way. Did she really want to go out sober, of all things?

She decided that no, she did not. Glancing at the sheeted windows and door of her kitchen, she hid the bottle in the same plantar in the front yard that she'd placed the gold bar, both of which would come in handy when the apocalypse hit. Then, she responded to Stuart with a single sentence—

> I'll have you know that there isn't a drop of alcohol inside this house

It was true, and she felt satisfied knowing the technicality of her response would annoy the hell out of him.

She texted her mother.

> I haven't found the piggy bank. It could have been thrown away in the chaos. It was falling apart anyway

This could go one of two ways—either Ma would accept the loss and grieve like a regular adult, or she would not accept it and spend the next two days panic texting Josie, worrying over how the plastic that her father once touched was now degrading in a landfill like some sort of filth and is that all her father's memory was worth to her? As if Josie didn't hold a shrine to his memory in her garage, boxes of random belongings labeled "Dad's stuff." Things she promised she'd sort through once she had the time. This had been one of the things Stuart had pressed hard for— you can't keep all this stuff in the living room, Josie. Then after, you can't keep all this stuff in the garage. When are you moving this stuff? You can't avoid it forever, you must move on.

Her memory of that time was as conflicted as grief itself— part rage, part guilt, part all-consuming sadness, the kind of sadness that threatened to darken every light she passed under.

Phone buzzing in her hand, she set it down without looking.

Ma just needed to tire herself out a bit. Josie would speak to her tomorrow, once both had some time to think about what they were going to say. They were similar in this regard.

On the upside, there was no better segue into work than to upset her mother. Her mood was already in the toilet, no better time to engage in customer service quicksand than now. No one could be better at making her feel terrible than her mother. Or Stuart. Or both. Shit, those two were like a sniff of preshow cocaine. May as well ride the high while it lasted.

A sense of familiar dread sank to her toes as the laptop whined to life. The sinking feeling occurred after every extended break from her work, that feeling of "why the fuck do I do this for a living?" followed by an intense desire to set her autoreply to a sparkly middle finger and set her computer on fire. This discomfort was one of the reasons she stuck to such a rigorous routine. If she didn't, she'd burn out spectacularly and then her only options for employment would involve seeing all these assholes in person. And if she thought her clients were terrible via email, the thought of looking them in the eye every day made her want to eat her arm off the bone.

She'd always been a pragmatist.

The queue blinked alive in front of her and it was every bit as panicked as she expected.

URGENT

URGENT

URGENT

A sea of non-urgent emails labeled urgent simply out of impatience. Josie was certain that literally nothing these people could need from her was urgent, yet here was urgency smeared across her usually polished queue.

Her first task was to compile her apology email, which needed to be blunt yet vague, brief yet explanatory.

I had some fucking personal problems, assholes. Calm down.

A good working draft, now to check her handy guide.

She went back and forth for an hour before finalizing her response, which was about fifty-eight minutes longer compiling a draft than usual. She struggled to categorize the past few days in a cogent way, unsure which personal crises to pinpoint—the skeleton thing or the vine thing or the drinking thing or the possibility of imminent destruction in a very short time. The point was that, of all persons involved in her work dealings, she was near the top of the list as far as bad days went. She surmised she might even be at the top of that list, but there was no way to know for sure. One could never guess how shitty someone else's life could really be, or what they were going through. Never.

She reread her response for a third time, before bcc'ing her entire client base. It read thusly:

Dear Valued Clients,

As many of you are aware, I have been briefly unreachable this past week. I could list all the reasons why that is, but at the end of the day we all know this will not come close to restoring your lost money, time, and trust; trust in both me and the service I provide. For that, I am deeply sorry. Life certainly has a way of upending itself just when you think you have it figured out.

For your trouble, I am offering each of you one free email consult, should you decide to use it. To redeem, please respond to this email with your request. I will make it my mission to reply to each of you within one business day. Additionally, if there is anything else I might do for you, please do not hesitate to ask.

Again, I apologize for any inconvenience these delays have caused, and I hope I might be able to restore your trust in me, one email at a time.

Kindly,
Josie

It was a nice little email. So nice that while she anticipated some blowback, she felt oddly assured it might just do the trick. Not everyone would be happy, no one ever was, but maybe the fallout wouldn't be quite as bad as she thought.

Staying true to form, it turned out she had no idea how wrong she was.

This was probably where she first strayed off course—instead of closing the laptop and steeling her nerves until regular business hours, she made herself a cup of tea while her inbox reliably dinged with responses.

Her second mistake was reading even one of these responses before having a nice drink warming her gut.

Some of the highlights included:

- Typical milenial response! (Millennial spelled incorrectly, of course)
- Personal issues don't excuse you for being in breach of contract! You'll be hearing from my lawyer shortly. I am out thousands of dollars.
- I lost three clients because I couldn't get a hold of you.
- I have already reported you to the better business bureau and left reviews on Google and Yelp. Don't use this company, it's nothing but a scam run by a liar.
- Convenient response after stealing my money!!!!!! I want a refund!

Her personal favorite—and it was near impossible to choose among them—came from her favorite/least favorite client of all.

- You're lucky you contacted me. I had just called my cousin, if you know what I mean—Jackie

None of this should have surprised her. None of it did, honestly, but she still found herself stuck to her seat in surprise. Not all the messages were bad—in fact, many wished her well and thanked her for reaching out. Most clients said nothing at all, which suggested they had already moved on, or didn't really care, or simply—and more astoundingly—*understood*. Then, there was the Jackies, the people who legitimately thought that an appropriate course of action to less than perfect customer service was to hire goons to inflict grievous bodily harm to the service provider, to stalk them to their home and punch them in the face. Granted, she knew Jackie well enough to know he was bluffing, yet to have the gall to actually speak these words to her while she was in the middle of a personal emergency, well, the lack of empathy was simply appalling. Then again, was she so different?

Without responding to any of them, she slammed her laptop shut and tapped nervous fingers on the tabletop. "I picked a fine day to try and stop drinking."

Po's ears perked but fell again after a moment. The house seemed dark and dreary, perhaps darkness was on account of her mood, or perhaps it was the sheets she'd pinned across the windows. The clock on the microwave blinked the time, one in the afternoon, but it felt like the twilight of morning in here. She should open a window, let the light in, but squatting in the back was Skelly, and Sue might catch her eyes if she opened the front.

Josie went to the closed front curtain to sneak a peek. If Sue was out then she'd just deal with the dreariness, but before she even touched the curtain her primal senses picked up on a wrongness. It took her a minute to figure out what it was—there was no light. Usually, an ambient, afternoon sun burned fluorescent through the curtains, but they were dark as night at one in the afternoon.

She pulled at the edges of the curtain, unsure what to expect. Letting the fabric drop back into place, she paused before allowing a deep sigh to escape. "This is ... interesting."

Po remained in his deep sleep, unconcerned with her current plight. He didn't even lift an ear as she raked the curtain across the rod, exposing a black window.

Vines.

Vines plastered against her window with such immaculate precision that not a drop of light broke through their barrier. With the flash of her phone, she traced their weave across the glass, a sensation that could only be described as monumental heartburn rising in her throat.

This was a problem. Skelly and her vines had always been a problem, but now they were a hyper-visible problem, and those were the type to invite all sorts of unwanted opinions into her life. Fuck, if she had even an ounce of patience for more of that.

As if on cue, there was a knock at the door—a casual, just-dropped-by-to-borrow-some-sugar kind of knock, which meant it was Sue. No one else could maintain such unconcern in the face of the disastrous state of her house.

Josie opened the door to Sue's passive expression. Both women just glared at one another for a bit.

"Things are going well," Sue said, indicating toward the window.

"It's under control."

"Sure."

The words came out before Josie could stop them. "Skelly didn't think much of your theories, by the way."

Sue laughed. "That's funny."

"What's so funny?"

"That you presume to know a lick of what Skelly thinks."

"She practically told me as much, right before snatching one of my darkest memories out of the ether and bleating it back to me like some sort of punishment. How would she know such a thing about me? The only way she could is by reading my mind or being there herself. But even then …"

There were many expected reactions to a comment like that, and none of them were for Sue to say, "Ah, that explains it."

Sensing Josie's confusion, Sue elaborated. "It explains the vines. Don't assume they'll stop coming, by the way. They'll gladly choke you to death."

"They can join the club then, I guess."

"Not your first time?"

"With murderous vines? Yes, but I suspect a lot of people I know wouldn't mind choking me to death."

It was a joke, of course, but Sue didn't seem amused. "Can I come in?" she asked instead.

There was a host of reasons to say no, and each of them screamed at her. "Sure."

"Really? Are you sure?"

"Do you want to come in or not?"

"I just didn't expect you to say yes." Sue scanned the room, a scowl like a bad smell sneaking onto her face.

"What are you looking for?"

"A man with a gun."

"I'm a hostage all right," Josie said.

"To whom?"

Josie leveled a glare in Sue's direction. "Ever since you and Skelly showed up, I've done everything in my power to keep you both out of my life, yet here we are—you in my living room and her with her stalker plants crowding my windows. You're like quicksand. Fighting only makes it worse."

"So, you're changing tactics. Smart."

Josie waved her toward the couch. "Yeah?" Anyone who liked cheesy movies as much as she did would know what happens when people step in quicksand.

Having Sue inside her home was weird. Her features were different here—the lines of her face darker, more prominent. She looked older, though that could also be due to the poor lighting.

Even Po was out of sorts. He hovered in the kitchen archway, sidelong glances ping-ponging between the women because for everything he'd seen these past few days, an actual guest inside this house was the strangest.

Sue soaked into the couch cushions, melting into their softness. "I do miss a good couch."

"You might try unpacking," Josie said, remembering the disheveled state of her house.

"Is there a couch in there I don't know about?"

"You could unpack, then, you know, go buy a new couch."

"Maybe I will." Looking as carefree as ever, Sue surveyed the room before settling defiantly on Josie's face.

"What do you want then?"

Sue clasped her hands together. "Seems you've made quite a mess of things, haven't you?"

"Is that what you came over here for? Because I can tell you that I have a perfectly good mother to make me feel like shit. I'm not sure I need another."

Sue laughed. "You could never be my daughter. I'd have absorbed you in utero."

"Charming," Josie responded, trying her damnedest to quell the surge of respect brimming in her chest. Throwing a person she respected out of her home was much more difficult.

And though Josie never asked, Sue continued. "I never wanted kids. Found out in my thirties that I couldn't have them anyway, which was a convenient conversation killer whenever pregnancy came up at parties, or holidays, or any place that shared attendance with a child."

"Nothing says 'change the subject' better than 'I'm barren.'"

"The declaration has come in handy once or twice."

Josie related, being a thirty-something loner herself, but instead of a biological wild card to defer judgment she simply double-fisted a couple of martinis at every social event until people stopped asking. She didn't actively dislike the idea of motherhood, but never really liked the idea of it either. Stuart had always asserted he wanted kids but would wait until she was ready, which was fine by her. Turned out to be one of the few wise decisions their marriage ever produced.

Regardless of their certainty, the topic still hung on the women's lips, each of them hesitant to shake it off. Babies had that affect whether a person cared for them or not. A life lived too long in the absence of a child was questioned, mourned, and pitied. Especially a woman's life. Especially a single woman's life. Even though Josie knew the argument was merely a bullshit byproduct of capitalistic patriarchy that needed her to make more tiny consumers, a sincere loss entwined itself within that emotional nest.

"So, what do you want?"

Sue shifted in her seat. "I've come to help. If you want."

"Help how?"

"Not everything is a trick, you know."

"That hasn't been my experience." A headache bloomed inside her head. Just the presence of Sue and her expert mix of antagonism and compassion was enough to make her bedridden with a migraine.

"I'm not surprised, considering how little company you keep."

Po circled Sue's feet, eventually settling himself next to her on the couch.

The absolute gall of that dog to betray her this way. "The fewer the people, the fewer the heartache. Simple math."

"Do you want my help or not?"

"You don't have to be mean."

"I don't have to be any which way about it. I can help you, probably only a small amount, but it's help. You can accept that help or not."

The question required a single syllable response—yes or no, and still, Josie couldn't bring herself to choose either word. Sue maintained a professional level of eye contact, all the while stroking the top of Po's head like a Bond villain.

As if suddenly remembering to check the turkey in the oven, Sue sprung to her feet, startling Po out of his reverie. "Okay then," she said.

Josie hadn't even decided. The nanoseconds Sue had allotted for decision-making was up and the woman was already at the front door before Josie could protest.

Because she'd made a choice. Because she desperately wanted help. Because she couldn't bring herself to say so aloud.

Instead of fleeing the house under a cloak of disappointment, Sue indicated for Josie to follow her into the yard.

Her predicament was worse than Josie thought—vines lurched over the top of her house, dangling like windchimes over the lip of the roof. Her street-facing window was completely gone under a knotted mess of green.

The sight multiplied the strength of her headache. She sweat through her shirt. "Why are they doing this? Why is Skelly doing this?"

Clearing away a spot of gravel with her foot, Sue knelt low to the ground. "Skelly isn't doing anything. These vines are listening to you. How do you think Skelly got here to begin with?"

She placed her hands over the small dirt spot, removing them to expose a bright green bud. This one was different than the flowers Josie had seen in her yard so many days ago, more delicate, thinner at the stalk. As Sue rose to her feet, so too did the bud, stretching to meet her until reaching the middle of shins. Then it bloomed, a fragile white flower unfurling toward the sun.

"How did you do that?"

Running gentle fingers over the petals, Sue turned to her.

"How do you breathe? It's hard to explain. It's just something I know how to do now."

"You mean to tell me that I've been controlling these ... vines?"

"That's the only reason they'd be here."

"But how? Genuinely, how? How did you come to control the flowers?"

Sue laughed, but sincerely instead of at Josie's expense. "I called them, and they came. I didn't understand how until I met Skelly, as you call her."

"And she explained everything to you, just like that?"

"Please, you've met her. I pieced it together with what I've learned over the years. Even now, I'm not sure how much of it is my own bullshit theory or actual truth. I suppose I'll never know for sure, but I'm okay with that."

Josie hunched over her knees, trying to come to grips with it all. "Years. She's going to live in my yard for years?"

"I doubt that. I've known her long enough to know this behavior is different. Her deal with you, the ferocity of these vines, her constant lingering in your yard. Something is happening, something big."

"Oh, that's just *super*."

"In the meantime, you need to get a grip, otherwise these vines will kill you."

"If I'm controlling them, wouldn't that be suicide?"

"Not exactly. They're listening to you, responding to you, but you aren't their master. They do have a will of their own and they will exercise that will if the situation gets too far out of control."

Josie righted herself a little too forcefully, jostling her equilibrium. "So, what am I supposed to do about it?"

"I keep telling you and you keep not listening. Ask them to leave."

"How the fuck am I supposed to do that? Whisper it in their vine ears? Scream at them? Hey, vines, get the fuck off my house!"

As she said it, the vines began to untangle from the window whipping away from the glass with the suddenness of electrocution.

"It's really that simple," Sue said. Then, waving her hand over the flower she summoned moments ago, it curled into itself and sunk back into the dirt as if having never been there in the first place.

"I've screamed these same words at Skelly a dozen times now and she's still here."

"She's different."

A few vines lingered in the shadows of the front walk-up. Josie waved them away, and to her evolving shock, they once again obeyed.

"See?" As soon as Sue said it, she froze in place. "Do you feel that?"

Josie listened as if she'd be able to hear the thing Sue had felt. "I don't feel anything."

"Skelly is here."

"Where?" Jose peered over her shoulder. "I don't see anything."

"You've noticed that she sort of floats in and out, yes? Well, she's in. You'll find her in your yard, I'm sure."

"Oh, that. She can sit on her throne all she likes."

"You think you're going to ignore her?"

"Think? I *am* ignoring her, thank you."

Josie turned away, ready to flee back inside when Sue snatched her by the shoulders. "She will consume you long before you successfully execute your point, Josie. Don't even try. She has an eternity of practice in patience."

"So, I just let her overrun my life until she takes whatever it is she wants from me? That's all anyone ever does, and then I'm left here holding a bill as long as a CVS receipt of emotional baggage that I have nowhere to put. And I've gotten used to it from the people in my life, but I don't know what I did to deserve it from something like her, too. All I wanted was to stay inside my little fucking house and live my little fucking life, but because she decides to pop in like a nosey tourist, I'm supposed to just bend over?"

Sue drummed her fingers on Josie's shoulders. "My, you really do love a good simile, don't you?"

"Excuse me—"

"Is that really what you want?"

This wasn't the question she expected. "I want to be left alone."

"Do you really? Or is that just easier?"

Josie shimmied out of her grasp. "What do you care anyway?"

Sue shrugged as casually as if being asked if she liked lemonade on a hot day. "I suggest you think about that. Then I suggest you go confront the skeletal demon in your yard before the strain of it kills you."

"If your relationship is any indicator, I have a few decades to decide what I want to say."

"If the deal you made is any indicator, then you really don't."

The sheets over her windows worked well at keeping Skelly out of sight and mind for the remainder of the day. After Sue left, Josie had considered her proposal of dealing with the situation head on for a proper thirty seconds, before deciding against it. Dealing with things has never been one of her strengths, and she wasn't compelled to start now. Instead, she yanked the vodka bottle out of the pot in her front yard and popped that puppy open for what she assumed would be one final hurrah. At this rate, she'd either be up to her eyeballs in plants or out of money and to let a good bottle of booze go to waste would be a shame.

As certain as she was, she couldn't help but choke back the guilt as the twist-off top cracked open. Stuart had been right after all. So had her mother, because she had been drunk last night and here she was getting drunk again. She *did* need to stop doing this for everyone's sake. Then again, they weren't here, were they? They didn't want her to stop for her own good, but for theirs, so she would stop being an inconvenience. So she would stop existing in the sad corners of their pasts. They wanted her to be content for them, no matter how she felt.

She poured a large glass, dropping a few ice cubes in to refine her drink a bit. The guilt was easy to ignore under the much heftier cloak of resentment. Nausea rose inside her chest as she chugged half the contents in a single pull, but that too was soon cast away by a dense warmth flowing outward from her gut to her fingers. This was the best part. If her habit of escalating bad ideas was any indicator, she would soon cease to be an issue for anyone besides a mortuary attendant.

"Bleak," she said to herself. "Things are getting dark over here, Po."

The dog trotted to her side, gazing at her with his saucer eyes—a perpetual mixture of agitation and devotion. She hadn't even considered him, her Po, in all this. Who would take care of him if something happened to her? Stuart would sooner take him to the pound, and her mother was unpredictable. Even under the best circumstances, the two of them would probably hate one another, and she couldn't do that to Po.

But that was just like her, finding all sorts of ways to chicken out of total personal destruction. There was always a reason—her family, her dog, taxes. Always something. Perhaps that's why she adopted Po to begin with—she needed a reason to keep putting feet to the pavement.

"What do you think about Sue?" she asked the dog, who upon not hearing the words "treat" or "food," quickly lost interest. Josie wasn't paying attention, though, and was now nose deep in her junk drawer searching for a notepad. Settling on a gas receipt she found smashed inside a pocket of her purse, she hastily scribbled a note with a black sharpie, her large handwriting funneling down in size as she ran out of space.

DEAR SUE, I KNOW THIS IS A STRANGE REQUEST BUT IF YOU FIND ME DEAD OR SOMETHING HAPPENS TO ME PLEASE TAKE PO THE DOG HIS MILKBONES R N PANTRY

She taped the note to the inside of her front door so anyone inside her house would see it.

"There," she said. "All set."

Then, she pounded back a large gulp of vodka. The competing elements of shame and a migraine and the warmth of the booze turned her stomach in knots, but the booze won out. Her problems were easy to forget under its lull. It was easy to ignore the way Po cocked his head as she bounced off the corners of tables and countertops. Easier still to push Stuart's text to the back of her mind, saving his disappointment for another day.

Picking up a glass became easier and easier, along with the ability to brush off the promise to quit she'd made to herself just hours prior. Then again, not much was more difficult than facing the realities of her life sober. She was a champion of avoiding reality.

She didn't remember her couch being so comfortable. Nor had she remembered the way it vaguely buzzed intermittently. The realization jolted her with adrenaline—her phone. This was a constant, rhythmic vibrating. Not a text, but a phone call.

Just as the call stopped it would start again. Someone was calling her repeatedly. Rage welted her skin at the sheer audacity. Who would be calling her? Probably Jackie, ready with a threat and a plea. Probably any variation of a Jackie—someone who paid her to actively dislike them. Someone desperate.

Like her.

Po leaped to the floor as she tossed couch cushions around the room. Her phone clattered to the tile along with them, and as she read the banner name of the caller, she froze.

Her mother.

The call died, voicemail pinging before the phone started ringing anew.

Ma was likely in the throes of a panic attack. This happened more frequently since Dad died, but her ardor could hardly be attributed solely to the loss. This was one of the reasons why Josie and her dad were such a dynamic duo, each sheltering the other from her mother's raging anxiety. They loved her, but facing her alone was like the slow bruise of a stubbed toe—a mere annoyance that mutated into a constant reminder of pain with every step.

This was not a call Josie could avoid, no matter how much she might want to.

"Hi, Ma," she said, bracing for her typical shotgun blast panic shouting.

"Josie, I'm so glad I finally reached you." Ma paused here, clicking her tongue to her cheeks as she presumably searched for words. "How are you?"

An odd direction for her mother, but Josie's canned response snapped to her mouth before she could stop it. "I'm fine, Ma."

"Okay."

"What's wrong?" Josie asked.

"I'm fine, honey."

Ma was clearly not fine. "Are you sure?"

"Yes! I said I was fine, didn't I?"

"Then why have you called me a dozen times in a row? Did the toilet block up again? Or are you really pressed for that helmet bank that I told you I can't find?"

"Those aren't the only reasons for a mother to call her daughter, but yes, I do want the bank if you ever find it."

Those were the only reasons *this* mother called *this* daughter, though.

"Well, I didn't find it."

"I know. You'd have told me."

"Then why are you calling?"

Ma let out a long sigh, beginning and stuttering out three sentences before they could get off the ground. She never did acclimate to Josie's brutal directness.

"I just want to know how you are."

"I'm fine, Ma—"

"No, how you really are."

Now, this was unusual. "What's going on, Ma? Is something wrong?"

"I don't know if something is wrong. That's why I'm calling."

"What does that mean?"

"It means I want you to tell me the truth."

God damn it. One evening of missed calls and now her mother was pressing her like a seasoned interrogator. Josie didn't possess enough of her usual willpower to lie to her, at least not successfully. "I'm fine. My phone was on silent last night and I didn't hear it. I'm obviously not dead. Just a little flighty."

"That's not why I'm calling."

Josie covered the receiving end of her phone as she whispered curses in Skelly's general direction. Even though the windows were covered and her words oozing quietly from pursed lips, something told her Skelly could hear her. Josie willed her to hear her curses. *You stealthy, boney bitch.*

"Then why *are* you calling?"

Another sigh, more exasperated than the last. "I wish you weren't so defensive all the time."

"That's why you're calling? To scold me?"

"Sometimes a mother hen just wants to check on her chick. Have you ever considered that?"

No. "Sure, I guess."

"I guess you wouldn't understand, anyway."

"Well, this has been loads of fun, but—"

"I got your auto-reply."

"What auto-reply?" Josie hadn't emailed her mother anything in years.

"Premium Client Unlimited's auto-reply. The email blast, or whatever you call it."

Josie didn't realize her mother knew what she did for a living, let alone the name of her company, let alone subscribed to her email blasts.

"What personal emergency?" Ma asked.

"Oh, that? I'd just fallen behind on some work and it was easier to say that than to admit I was being lazy." Josie's palms were suddenly sweaty.

"You are many things, dear daughter, but lazy has never been one of them. What is really going on?"

"Nothing."

"You aren't a liar either. Not a good one, anyway."

Just who was this woman? "Did you hit your head on the docks or something?"

"Stop trying to redirect, Josie. Something is wrong. A mother knows her daughter. I know *you*, no matter how much you protest."

She felt the tide pushing against the dam wall, and she was fixing to split down the middle. What would mother dearest think of the truth? She'd probably get in the car before she'd even hung up the phone and be on her doorstep tomorrow, ready to have her daughter committed. But then she'd see. Josie could shove her headfirst into the backyard and give her a face to face with her eminence, wreaker of havoc and mayhem, Miss Skelly the Skeleton herself.

"It's really nothing, Mom. Just some stupid shit and I got a little lax with work. You saw the email. I'm back at it again, just like normal."

"No, you aren't."

"And how exactly would you know?"

"Because I emailed you."

"Emailed me what?"

"A request. Through your website. I wanted to … make sure."

"Well, it is a Sunday."

"That's never stopped you before."

A wide silence settled over the women. It was many minutes before either of them spoke.

"Wait. You're a client? How many times have you emailed me? You've paid money to email me bogus claims? Am I hearing this right?"

There was a moment of hesitation more before her mother admitted to the ruse. "I'm not a golden client, or whatever you call it. It wasn't that much money."

"What did you ask me?" Josie asked. All her relationships were hotter garbage than she expected.

"Honestly, I don't even remember. I made it up. I wanted to

know what it was you did."

Josie wasn't the only terrible liar in the family. She wagered her mother could recite those emails from memory right now if she wanted to. "Why didn't you just ask me?"

"I tried. I don't know. I can never ask you anything unless I'm prepared to fight. I didn't want to fight with you."

Well, wasn't that just adorable? This coming from the mother who fled the state the second Dad died. The one that commandeered the boat, gutting all those memories and replacing them with a dusty trinket memorial to Dad. The woman who sits alone in her sad crypt, only reaching out to her daughter when she needs something from the boxes she abandoned in Josie's garage. How convenient to leave her kid in the bottom of a collapsing grave and then blame her for being bitter as she's buried alive.

"I have to go," she said, measuring her tone so as not to inflame the situation even more.

"Don't do that. I'm sorry, I didn't mean it like that, it's just … we never were very good at talking to one another."

"I know, Ma. So, I'm stopping now before things get out of hand. It's for the best."

"Josie, I lo—"

She hung up before her mother could finish her sentence. No matter what she might say, Ma could never give what Josie wanted. They were too different. They'd had decades of damage and unsaid things to unravel, and Josie was not prepared to deal with any of it now.

To her eternal relief, Ma didn't bother dialing her back. Thank God for simple pleasures.

Cramming more booze down her throat, she logged into her email and began the hunt for her mother's phony account. She'd already told her she wasn't a gold member so that just left the hundreds of one-off clients she kept in a separate folder to hit up whenever she was low on cash. One of those accounts belonged to Ma, and she was determined to figure out which one and block it.

This, as it turned out, was a much bigger task than anticipated. She started by searching predictable keywords like her mother's name—Carol, which she hated—her father's name—Bob—widow, mother, ma, boat, dock, Josie's name, anything about porcelain doll collectibles—her mother's former obsession—and her dad's favorite baseball team. Each time there was a match, she'd have to read through the email and search for clues from her mother. The woman couldn't possibly have been so stealthy that Josie couldn't figure out her code. Knowing her, she probably asked how to get a distant "employee" to purchase a plane ticket to San Diego and help her fix the toilet on her boat. No, Josie would have figured that out on sight. Damn, maybe she shouldn't have had more to drink until after she was done sleuthing.

There might be an easier way.

Just as Sue predicted earlier, Skelly perched atop her throne, skull resting against a curled fist. Casual as ever, as if this was all a slightly boring game to her.

The vines Josie had just cast away laid themselves before her as she opened the back door, oozing out of the way of her feet as she strode toward Skelly, stopping at the base of the throne.

"What's her email?"

"*Good afternoon, Little Bird.*"

"What email did she use?"

"*Whose email?*"

"You know exactly what I'm talking about."

"*I'm not sure what you take me for, but I am not your obedient crystal ball.*"

"Did you get inside my mom's head just like you got into mine? Convince her to join the mailing list, to email me at work, and pretend? You'd have her pay me just to have the benefit of a response?"

"Sounds to me like your mother is just as desperate as you are. Despite your best efforts, you are more like her than you think."

Josie wasn't thinking. Or maybe she was, just not clearly. Emotion much vaster than fury bubbled to the surface. She snatched at Skelly's cold forearm, squeezing as hard as she could.

"Remove your hand immediately."

"Just tell me what I want to know, and I'll leave you alone."

"Release my arm, child. This will not end well for you."

She squeezed harder, though the pressure was of little consequence to Skelly. "None of this has gone well for me. Not one fucking thing. What's one more? What's one more bad thing, Skelly, tell me!"

"Fine."

Josie didn't have time to react before the ground below her began to seize. She fell backward as the ground ripped apart, a cavernous tear in her yard splitting her and Skelly apart by a matter of six feet or more. Tiled shingles shattered to the ground as her house wobbled unsteadily, the earth below it shifting like sand in a storm. Somewhere inside the house, Po wailed, a howl she hadn't heard since his first lonely night in her home— an instinctual terror. Josie felt the same way but was too busy scrambling to safety to make any noise.

When it all settled, Skelly remained as impassive as ever on her throne. The block wall separating Josie and Sue's yard had conveniently crumbled.

"You see, Little Bird, there is something we skeletons consider gospel. An ironclad rule to which we are all bound, and you'll do well to listen. It's called consent, and we only tolerate one violation."

And for once—for once—Josie was speechless. The whirling accusations, the what-about-me's, the unbridled rage, was all zapped out of existence. Her fear wasn't because of the gaping tear in the earth or the raw power unleashed without so much as a gasp—it was because Skelly was right.

All that other shit was terrifying, too, obviously, but nothing was scarier to her than witnessing how easily she could undo herself. How quickly she could become the type of person she hated.

She wasn't aware of the severity of her trembling until the vines came for her. Creating a bridge of themselves, they laced their way toward her, sidling up against her back so she could maintain her protective, fetal position. With one final clap, another roof tile swung toward the concrete, shattering. Otherwise, the world was silent. Everything. Not even Po was barking anymore.

Before the worry could swell, Skelly held up a hand to silence her. It was the most she'd seen her move since their ceremonious handshake, and even this was different. Before, the hand had lurched out as if operated by a lever. She swayed now with the familiar grace of one burdened by being alive—fluidity restrained by muscles and sinew and physics.

"You hear it, don't you?"

"I don't hear anything."

Skelly nodded as if this was the correct answer.

"I'm sorry. I shouldn't have grabbed you like that." And she *was* sorry.

"You should have let go when I asked."

"Is Po ...?"

"I wouldn't hurt your dog. Give me a little credit. Besides, we tend to bend the rules for the ones we like."

Skelly had gone still again, either retreating to her normal stoicism or deeply considering Josie in a way she'd never done before.

"He's never this quiet."

"Nor is he now, you just can't hear him. But that does not mean he is quiet. For that matter, neither are you."

To this, Josie might have previously objected, but Skelly was hinting at something, and she wanted to know what it was before this hole swallowed her up, and her little dog, too.

"Allow me to tell you a story, Little Bird."

Skelly leaned into her throne, leg resting comfortably across the opposite knee.

"Once upon a time, there was a woman who lived in a little village called Nowhere. It was an isolated plot of land existing far off any map you might have studied, yet the people thrived due to the endless forest that surrounded the village. With its bounty they harvested fruits and nuts, hunted game, gathered wood for shelter and tools, eventually creating a healthy bartering system amongst the townspeople. This woman's name was Noone, and she was born of a line of skilled weavers. Every morning she would venture into the sacred woods in search of a threading tree, named so due to their cloud-like blossoms that could be spun into yarn, completely unique to its world. You see, threading trees were near invisible. They grew only in the shadows of the densest portion of the woods, the places sunlight never touched, yet could only be exposed by the glint of sunlight along their leaves. Like her mother before her, Noone traversed to the darkest parts of the wood, the most dangerous, the places of poison and blind things and black moss, and called to the threading trees, for Noone was among the few to know their proper name."

The vines shifted underneath Josie's body, pushing her upright before snapping into the shape of a low-hanging tree with wispy leaves much like that of a weeping willow. The tree soon consumed everything—Skelly, the yard, the sun, her house. She was like a mouse underneath its magnificent umbrella, and as she marveled, its branches began to quiver as if carried by a breeze.

"Do you know what that name was?"

Josie patted the roots made of vines, tracing her finger

along their path at her feet. The answer came to her just then, as suddenly as if someone had blurted it out loud. "Sister," she said. "Their name was sister."

"Yes. Every morning, Noone would sing to her sisters, a song only they understood, for only if they swayed under a break in the forest canopy could Noone see the blossoms that dropped in their wake."

"This must be some epic yarn to go through all this trouble," Josie said, squinting through the cracks in the leaves in the hopes of catching a glimpse of a blossom. She saw none.

"Oh, yes. Remarkable. Unlike any that exists today. This yarn, when spun into garments, would meld with the desires of the wearer. The same cloak worn by one might present as a long, glittering gown to another, perhaps a suit of armor to a third. But these garments took years to fashion. It was considered a rite of passage among the adults to receive their otherwise invisible garments, and they wore them proudly, every day, often until the day of their death."

The leaves of the tree sunk lower to the ground so the sun only broke through in small peeks.

"What did Noone's garment look like?"

"Noone never wore one."

"Why?"

"Would you wear the skin of your sisters on your back?"

"I might if it looked anything like I am imagining."

"You lie, Little Bird. But if you challenge my assertion, you could surely ask her yourself."

Josie pulled away from the trunk of the tree. "How?"

With those words, the tree dissolved, vines stripping themselves from their design as they unraveled from the top down, in the end leaving all but one small tendril curled around Josie's shoes.

"There she is."

"You're pulling my leg."

"*I am not, as fun as that might have been. Neither of us have the time.*"

"This is Noone? The woman from another world that spun invisible thread into make-believe ball gowns?"

"*They were not make-believe, but yes, that is her.*"

The vine at her feet corkscrewed itself up her leg, pausing at Josie's knee. The sight of it might have frightened her, but she didn't detect any malice in the movement.

"Are you Noone?" Josie asked. The vine tightened its grip only a moment, then relaxed.

"Holy shit!" she said, yanking her leg free.

The tendril disappeared into the mass, undecipherable from the others once again.

"*These are our stories, Little Bird. Each of them the exact moments when we became what we are.*"

"I thought they were fairy tales."

"*They are.*"

"But you're telling me they're real."

"*Whoever made you think they weren't real?*"

"Reality. Logic."

"*Whose reality and logic? Yours?*"

"Well, yes. The collective logic. Human logic."

Skelly waved off this notion with a snap of the wrist.

"*Short-sighted.*"

"I suppose, but until now it's all I've known."

"*Know more, then.*"

"Teach me, then."

"*What do you think I've been trying to do?*"

Josie got to her feet, dusting the bits of rock and dirt off her clothes. "Drive me insane."

"*You needed no help there, Little Bird. Surely you must know that much.*"

She wasn't quite ready to concede, so she left the barb alone and slunk her body under the shade of her patio now hanging at uneven angles, threatening collapse at any second. Gesticulating toward her roof, she said, "This doesn't help."

"*Structural integrity is of little consequence today.*"

"That's right. Our deal. I haven't much time left, do I?"

"*Neither of us do.*"

"What is going on, Skelly? What is going to happen at the end of our time together?"

"*That depends entirely on you.*"

Speaking to Skelly was the most exhausting act of Josie's life. Worse than speaking with her mother. "How did I know you were going to say that?"

"*Perhaps you aren't as resistant to an education as I thought.*"

Her house let out a distressing groan, the foundation surely all sorts of fucked.

"*I look forward to your story, Little Bird.*"

Skelly lifted a hand as if to wave, and with an ethereal pop, she was gone. All the chatter of the world returned the second she was out of sight. Po's hysterics shattered the sound barrier, and she rushed inside to check on him. Physically, he was unharmed, but he was trembling as if just escaping the jaws of a crocodile. Patting his little head, she carried him into the backyard so she could properly survey the damage.

Dust still billowed in every direction, having yet to settle. She heard shouts from over the fence as various neighbors stumbled out of their homes in shock. Distant sirens pierced the air. The concrete debris of the shattered brick wall between her and Sue's homes clattered as a figure sauntered over the rubble and into her yard.

"Well, well, well," Sue said, expression slipping to the side of her face as she scowled. "You're more of a mess than I thought."

An earthquake has struck the metro area today—a magnitude of 6.0—causing minor damage throughout the region. Mr. John Smitherson of the United States Geological Survey has stated that the earthquake is extremely puzzling. So far, experts have been unable to locate the originating fault line as no such shocks have been reported in any fault-adjacent cities. "Shocks like this, while rare, are not unheard of," says Smitherson. "They are usually caused by the sudden release of gasses from underground magma reservoirs, though this has yet to be confirmed in this particular situation."

When asked if residents should expect any aftershocks, Smitherson states it is likely, however none to the same degree of the initial shock.

Josie read this out loud to Sue, who had just finished steeping another small pot of green tea. Po sniffed around her empty living room, appalled by the lack of furniture on which to sit.

"Clever," Josie added, simultaneously relieved and alarmed. At least the authorities patrolling the area hadn't yet zeroed in on her house, nor had any of the neighbors. Here was the confirmation Josie had been searching for since Skelly's arrival. She was not crazy. Skelly was real. This was no longer just some shared delusion between two lonely women.

"I doubt Skelly had much to do with it," Sue said, placing a teacup in front of her.

"Wouldn't she, though? To keep prying eyes away from her handiwork, at least until she's done torturing me like a bored house cat."

Josie sipped her tea without removing her nose from the screen of her phone. "It's all over Facebook and Twitter, too.

People felt it as far as King Creek."

"That's almost fifty miles."

"Yeah," she said, locking her phone. "How long before they trace it back to me?"

"I'm not sure."

"They're going to think I'm some sort of domestic terrorist looking to blow up the neighborhood with underground bombs or something."

"Well, there won't be any evidence of that, would there?"

Much in the manner of Skelly herself, Josie waved away the response with a flick of her wrist. "As if that matters."

"So, what are you going to do?" Sue watched her over the rim of her teacup, her stare intense and penetrating.

Josie wrapped her fingers around her cup. "Does she seem different to you?"

"How do you mean different?"

"You mentioned before that our deal was unusual. Is this unusual, too? Or can every wacky environmental hiccup be traced back to our friendly, neighborhood skeleton?"

Sue shifted in her seat as if rapidly sorting through all her potential responses. "That's hard to say. I guess I wouldn't know."

"But what do you *think*?"

"I think ... I don't know what I think."

"Yes, you do."

Sue dropped her cup, studying Josie closely.

"You can tell me the truth," Josie said. "It's too late for me to lose my mind."

"Well," she patted the table as if to grab something, but finding it missing instead fiddled with the tea handle. "I think something big is going to happen. Something that affects even her. She seems almost conflicted. Uncertain. Until now I've never witnessed her to be anything but perfectly assured."

"So, she's never ripped your property into two pieces?"

"Not mine, no."

The air smelled vaguely of smoke and gasoline, the familiar cologne of catastrophe. The tea, however, was lovely.

"I am the lucky one."

"Maybe," Sue said. "Or maybe just the last."

"Well, that would make infinitely more sense. I am definitely a last resort sort of character."

"Self-deprecation doesn't suit you like you think it does."

"I wasn't aware it served anyone like they thought it did."

"Only the rare few that know how to wield it without sounding pompous or pathetic." Sue topped up their cups, letting the spout of the teapot linger over Josie's cup until nothing but drips came out.

"I'll not ask which you think I am."

Whether from the tea or the trauma, Josie felt at ease in Sue's beautiful yard. The flowers looked brighter, too. Bigger. It was peaceful here. If not for this new bloom of frustration, she might have asked to stay a bit longer. Sue probably would have preferred her to stay here, considering the way she tittered and clucked over her. Sue was worried. Despite her best efforts, she couldn't keep the anxiety off her face.

Josie stood. "I should go."

"Your house is stable enough?"

"I think so. If it smothers me in my sleep, then we'll know for sure." She was sorry to leave the tea, but she needed to get some ibuprofen in her system fast.

"If things get worrisome, you can always stay here. At this rate, I'll be up all night." She indicated to the tea, and Josie nodded.

"I'll keep that in mind."

Po lunged at her, pawing ferociously at her jeans, thrilled by the prospect of escape. He didn't like Sue's barren house. She'd have to make a note to the request taped to her front door. *P.S. GET MORE FURNITURE*

For whatever hopes she held for this small headache, all were abandoned by the time she reached her own front door. This headache blossomed with deadly force, the likes of which she hadn't seen in years. Two years to be exact. She was never prone to migraines, or so she thought, until such a time in her life that her brain thought it prudent to mimic her bad fortune—the moment her life split in two, so did her head. There were all sorts of symbolism involved here, as well as a bit of chemistry and a lot of booze, but the coincidence couldn't be ignored. She'd been spinning her wheels endlessly for days, stalling in the mud once the vodka kicked in, only to push it into high gear again with the thrust of a fresh hangover. She was damn good at exacerbating misfortune, which was how she knew this migraine was going to be a biggie.

Po, for all his impatience, must have sensed the incoming blot to her senses with the acuity only a dog could possess. He followed her so closely that she continually kicked his snout with her shoes, determined to be underfoot even to his own detriment. He was also silent. She flopped onto her couch, the full weight of the last few days crushing her so deep into the cushion that she feared she might suffocate. A hollow fear—she was never that lucky.

Drifting in and out of a pained sleep, she was roused to an occasional consciousness by Po who continually licked her exposed ankles. She felt like an infant coaxed to breathing by an anxious mother, surely never something her own mom did for her. Not even as a newborn. Ma loved her, sure, but she was never much of the motherly type. And it showed. Such as in kindergarten, she told Josie it was unseemly for little girls to cry. Or after Josie socked the neighbor boy in the face for calling her freckles ugly and was sent to her room without dinner since girls should never be so aggressive. The lack of maternal instinct showed when Dad tried to hug Josie at graduation and Ma split them apart by the sheer force of her glare. It showed again when Ma would only extend a hand to her when she needed help carrying groceries from the car, or to swat Josie away from the orange tic-tacs in her purse.

But the worst of them all was when Dad died and she took off in the boat, squatting in the one place she could never claim dominance while he was alive. The lack was evident in all the ways mother and daughter tore at the seams of a perpetually awkward relationship—death by a thousand cuts.

She was laughing now, thinking about how stupid it all sounded. She was face down on her couch, cackling at nothing but her petty memories. Adding up every grievance now seemed so inconsequential. Decades of resentment, of weirdness, of distance, and all for what? They got along fine enough if Dad was there to play the buffer, and once he died all that was left between them was the vastness of their inability to relate to one another without him. Which meant every time they spoke, they were forced to confront his absence, rendering an already stiff exchange intolerable.

So, they didn't speak. A silent agreement formed between them, whether they acknowledged it or not. *You make this worse, so I guess we'll occasionally text each other so no one can accuse us of not trying.*

Thinking of her parents was difficult because of the migraine, because of emotions, and Josie fought the urge to pry her eyeball out with a spoon as the headache got comfortable in her right orbital sinus cavity. There was no way to stop it now. Once the migraine took residence behind the eye the only recourse was a nap and a prayer. Not even her powdered headache medicine, made specifically for such an occasion, could combat the pain.

Every time this happened, she swore she'd stop behaving

this way. Every time she reeled in pain because of her bad decisions, crippling herself, she assuaged herself by saying this was the last time. She was going to change.

"Things" was a good word for it—vague, but with enough specificity that she could momentarily feel better about herself. Things would be different once she changed them. Once she made an effort. There was only one problem to ideals like these—and that problem was her.

She'd almost sobered up once. Stuart had given her an ultimatum—drinking or him. He claimed he loved her, he said he wanted to be with her, but he couldn't if she continued to behave the way she was. She'd usually respond how he was too uptight. He used to go out as much as she did when they met, but somewhere along the way, he decided for the both of them that their electric lifestyle was too much and that they needed to grow up and settle. Josie had hated that word. He'd made sobriety sound like prison. And it wasn't as if she'd wanted to go and get blasted every night—she'd never taken to narcotics and hangovers well, as her present condition more than indicated, but she grew bored. She realized their life had cooled. The magic was gone, along with the street food cuisines and pop-up art installations and five-mile walks at night. The nights of walking because they had nothing else to do because all they wanted to do was feel the night wind on their cheeks and listen to one another talk unrestricted—those nights had been replaced by meals for two crockpot recipes and movie streaming. Which was fine, mostly, if not a bit stale. And for every organic, locally sourced, six-dollar carrot Stuart brought home from the farmers market to puree, she would top off her wine glass a little more. Good wine to go with good food she would say, but the narrative morphed over time.

If we are just going to stay in, I might as well enjoy a drink or two.

Or three.

Or more.

Until words were no longer necessary, and she was too drunk to remember them anyway. Sometimes she'd go on walks by herself, which was when she considered the idea of a dog, so she didn't look like a prowler casing the neighborhood at ten at night, but Stuart refused. He never explicitly said why. She had her theories, though, such as she was too much of a useless drunk to oversee anything, or that he'd wanted kids and was afraid that a dog would be enough for her and she'd never consent to them, or that maybe if he starved her for affection, she'd cave to whatever he wanted. Maybe she'd straighten out, come around to his way of thinking—the correct way, though he never stated so. Instead, he found himself over preparing his meals by half, while she roamed the neighborhood with a brown bag over her Chardonnay, desperately wishing she had someone to talk to, even if it was only a dog.

Then came the ultimatum, and her recovery. She didn't drink for eight months. Stuart was ecstatic. He made plans now that she was fixed. There were small portions of happiness then, and Josie figured maybe the problem was her all along. Maybe crushing boredom was her lot in life. Surely Stuart had sacrificed when they'd gotten married? Sometimes she wondered what that sacrifice had been, on those days when she was staring listlessly out the window like a doped-up Stepford wife, but she was too afraid to ask. Because she knew exactly what—who—it was.

Then, her dad got sick, and the marriage fell apart for good.

The irony was, now that he'd left her, she'd finally become nearly everything he'd ever wanted her to be.

Her life would be funny if it wasn't also so pathetic.

She blacked out soon after, unaware of the shadow creeping over the world as she did.

DAY EIGHT

SHE AWOKE. THOUGH groggy, the thought of remaining one extra second laying on the couch made her skin hurt. She'd been doing a lot of that lately. Blacking out and waking up delirious just to relive the same five seconds of realization repeatedly. The déjà vu was grating.

Po spun himself as she dragged herself off the couch for a glass of water. She fed him, adding a milk bone to the top for his trouble.

Silence crackled a static hum throughout the house. No sirens, no whoosh of passing cars in the distance, not even the expected occasional whoop and cry from the neighborhood kids that plagued the streets on evenings like this. Was it evening? She ought to check just to make sure she hadn't skipped more than a few hours in her stupor.

She opened her front door to what was precisely the middle of the night, knowing so by the pureness of the air. There was something about the hours just beyond midnight that had a settled quality to it. The sky shimmered a mix of purples and grays and blues, radiated to brilliance by a confident moon. Not even a city bursting of light could tamp it down, not at this hour.

Josie liked this time of day the most. Here she could think. Here she wouldn't be interrupted.

"Rest well?"

Josie was startled at the noise. Sue leaned within the frame of her own door, wistfully gazing into the night.

"I shouldn't be surprised to find you awake," Josie said.

The women whisper-shouted at one another, loud enough to be heard but in a way that eavesdroppers would understand they meant to be quiet, even though they were yelling across their respective lawns. This being preferable to moving.

"Rested quite well, it seems." She had yet to steal her eyes from the sky, which was pointedly obvious from a woman who never resisted an opportunity to stare at Josie until she collapsed into herself.

"I take it I missed something."

"Yes, but it's difficult to say what."

For some reason, Josie felt it prudent to check on her gold bar. "Something to do with our friend, I take it?"

"Not exactly," Sue said, hoisting herself upright. "I think something to do with hers."

"I wasn't aware she had any friends. Besides us, I guess."

Sue erupted into an uncontrolled cackle worthy of the witchiest storybook witch. "You don't have enough time to be this dense."

"Funny, but I think I've been told that before."

Sue nodded. "Where do you think I heard it?"

"You've been listening?" Josie wasn't expressly angry nor shocked. Sue had her part in this somehow, even if she didn't feel up to revealing its intricacies to her all at once.

"Not in the way you're thinking, Josie. I wouldn't do that to you." The way she spoke, Josie was sure she meant it.

"Why wouldn't you? You barely know me. Who cares?"

"You care, even if you won't admit it. I do, too." Sue knelt to a stoop over a patch of dirt. The way she summoned a flower from the barrenness, backlit by the moon, reminded Josie of the saltwater taffy pullers at the little shop she and her dad used to go to after boat trips. The sugar just aching for their hands, stretching out toward warm skin with desperate zeal.

"They communicate," she said. "In their own way. And not like you're thinking. They aren't little recorders. More like stamps. They imprint on everything they touch. The collective memory these tendrils possess is astounding."

"Skelly insinuated the vines used to be people."

"Did she?"

"I mean, in the way Skelly says anything. I never can tell when she's messing with me."

"I've not known her to outright lie, but she does omit convenient details at an alarming rate." Sue stroked the white petals of her flower, cooing it back into the ground.

"A roundabout sort of honesty." Josie understood. It was the only sort of honesty she subscribed to, finding it a sufficiently non-aggressive way to force people out of asking her things. She worked hard to make herself impossible to talk to. "I have a theory."

"About Skelly?" Sue asked.

"About you."

She had Sue's full attention now, a feat Josie realized she'd never yet achieved only now that she had. Despite Sue's seemingly oppressive attention, there was always an ambiguous distance to her. Josie had just never noticed until now.

"I think whatever deal Skelly's made with me, she made with you first. And I think you turned her down."

The one side of Sue's mouth—presumably the annoyed side—puckered into itself as the accusation stagnated between them.

"It wasn't a deal. Nothing like the bizarre dynamic you two have arranged."

Josie gripped the door to steady herself. "Whatever it was, you refused her in some way." The absence of a rebuttal was all the confirmation Josie needed. "Do you regret declining?"

"Does it matter?"

"Your answer would shed a clearer light on why you're here, sprouting flowers in the middle of the night with me, instead of being out there in the world, living a regular life."

"What would you call a regular life?"

"Oh, I don't know." Josie was going to start listing off items, the first of which is a husband and kids, instantly catching herself perpetuating the same cycle used against her. What exactly was a regular life? Because what came to mind immediately reminded her of the one she'd shunned and driven into the dirt until it was dead.

"I guess it was a stupid question."

Sue let a breath escape she must have been holding for a while. "No, it wasn't. But to answer you honestly, I guess I'd have to say I don't know if I regret it. Sometimes I think I do. Most days I think I do, but then, at times like these, when the night is quiet and I can really think ... Well, I think I made the right choice. Even with the regrets. It was right."

Neither woman had ventured beyond their respective doorsteps. This was a dangerous conversation, and each of them clung to the safety of their own space, only tossing their poisonous truths to one another from a distance.

"So, you follow Skelly around like a groupie or something?"

Sue cocked her head to the side, eyes narrowed.

Josie tossed up her hands. "Well, what are you doing here then?"

"Let me ask you something," Sue said, dangling a foot over her stoop as if to come closer, and reeling it in again when she seemingly thought better of the idea. "Has my presence helped?"

"Yes." She'd probably have died the other night without her. Just kept drinking and drinking until the vines crushed the life out of her. Instead, this strange, fanny pack connoisseur of a woman stood next to her in the rain, shaking her by the shoulders until she'd gotten enough of her shit together to arrive safely back inside.

And all this time Josie had been thinking of her as a nuisance.

"How many others have there been?" she asked.

"As many as it takes."

"As many as it takes to do *what*?"

Sue smiled now, which filled Josie with a satisfaction she hadn't experienced since she'd adopted Po. "As many as it takes to be right." Then the moment was gone, Sue's regular toothiness returning. "You should really read the news more, you know."

Not allowing for any sort of follow-up questions, Sue offered a curt nod before slipping back inside her home.

Po, comfortable enough in Josie's tentative lucidity, had already snored himself into a deep sleep on the couch. She joined him, stroking his ears softly enough to not disturb him. The night was nice, despite everything.

Had she known what was going to happen, she'd have tried to enjoy it more, but in that moment, her life was utterly perfect.

Josie was only partially awake when a knock rattled her backdoor. Po, immensely distressed, vaulted toward the door.

Josie groaned. "No," she said. "Go away."

Another knock answered her. The plates in her cabinets shuddered from the power of the incessant banging. It was a miracle the glass didn't shatter.

Josie felt out of control. The knocking kept coming. It wouldn't stop until she answered, and Po was furious.

"Go away," she repeated.

Her request was denied.

She had no choice but to answer lest she be serenaded with

poundings until she died. As she finally gave in, a swath of vines slithered away from the patio, having knocked on Skelly's behalf.

"I'm afraid we don't have the luxury of lazy mornings, Little Bird."

Josie grimaced as she stepped into the sunlight of her battered patio. "I was sleeping."

"That's nice."

"What do you want?"

Skelly reclined in her throne, fingers drumming against the sides. Josie parted her legs to allow Po to squeeze through. He bounded into her broken yard, wary of the sudden crevasse cut down the center. Her last, half-drunk bottle of vodka sat conspicuously on her counter, radiating shame and weakness that flushed her cheeks.

"Do you feel the earth trembling yet?"

Josie gazed around her destroyed yard, settling on the roof shingles piling on her cracked patio. "I have no idea what you're talking about."

"We're running out of time."

Josie peeled the edges of her nails until her fingers bled. "So?"

"Just thought you'd like to know."

"Thanks, that helps." The spectacular nature of all this was finally starting to settle, so much so it felt normal. A distressing amount of normal.

Crushing disappointment was not long to follow. There were so many directions for this series of events to land.

She had everything she'd always thought she'd wanted—intrigue, novelty, mystery. There couldn't possibly be a more interesting character to speak with than Skelly, and still she wanted nothing more than to run inside and ignore her.

So, while she was exhausted and aching, she had to resist her usual urge to flee. Clearly, fleeing wasn't working anyway. She had to try and do something right. Actually *trying* was the absolute, very least she could do. Purposeful action was also a terribly foreign concept to her. She winced, thinking about her past self.

"I take it you're still waiting for that story."

"Have you got one?"

Nope, she thought. "I think so," she said.

Skelly propped her skull atop the triangle of her hands.

"You don't have it."

"I must have something or else why would you be here?" This was more a reassurance to herself than a verifiable fact, but conjecture was all she had.

"Desperation."

Clearing her doorstep, she broached the lip of the patio. The sun was hot and bright and everything she hated about sunlight. "If that's the case, both of us are fucked."

"I'd wager this is true."

"Super," she said.

The two were quiet then, sizing up the other and individually deciding which of them was more pathetic. Unbeknownst to one another, they'd each decided this would be Josie.

"No one has ever tasked me with something like this. What is there to tell? I live alone. Chased away my partner. My dad is gone, and my mom nuked herself into grief on the boat, which coincidentally was the primary thing about our old lives that she hated the most. So, what is there to say? I'm nothing but a ghost these days. A ghost looking for a nice place to stay dead."

Skelly considered this long enough for Josie to wonder whether she was rethinking her decision to come here at all.

"Do you know what I like most about stories?"

"No, but I would be *delighted* if you told me."

"They never mean what you think they mean. They're puzzles, constantly scattering against the breath that births them."

"That explains a lot," Josie said, sitting with her back to one of the more stable patio columns. "About you, I mean."

"*Does it?*"

"You have a very purposeful way of speaking, saying exactly what you mean but in the most incomprehensible way possible. And I have no idea how to decode it, which is probably why I'm having such a hard time giving you what you asked for."

Skelly remained frozen over her hands, but the vines shifted as if suddenly disturbed, the same way Josie had that time a sewer roach crawled over her foot in the shower. For a moment, she could have sworn she heard them scream. Then again, she was probably projecting. She did that a lot—projecting her own backward emotions into other people's mouths.

Alert, the vines writhed along the base of Skelly's throne. They were excitable if that could be a word attributed to plants.

"*What exactly do you think I've asked for, Little Bird?*"

She knew she'd answered wrong before she'd even finished speaking, but that didn't stop her. "A story."

"*No.*"

Skelly's voice boomed underneath Josie's skin with paralyzing force. She was pretty sure her heart stopped. "My story," she said.

"*What about you do you assume I don't already know?*"

"I assume you know everything."

"*Everything?*"

"Am I wrong?"

"*In a way, you are.*"

"How am I wrong?"

"*I know events, Little Bird. I know what has happened to you. I've seen it a thousand times. People are not new, and no cleverer in their abuses than the generation before them, nor those before that. We are a simple species to our core.*"

Josie shifted her stance, catching the barest of admissions. "We?"

"*Well, of course. What would you think I am besides human?*"

She gesticulated to herself as if to highlight the obvious humanness of her skeleton.

"You may have been human once, but not anymore."

"*Why is that?*"

"Human skeletons don't reanimate and live for centuries beyond their flesh."

"*Yet here I sit.*"

A silence passed between them. Skelly leaned against the back of her throne, hands clutching the end caps of her armrests. Josie hadn't noticed these new growths until they were smothered underneath that boney grip.

"May I ask you something?" Josie asked after considerable time had slipped past.

"*You may.*"

"What would you—a mortal you—have called your current immortal self? What name would have prescribed to this visage?"

Skelly drummed her fingers over the snow pure buds.

"*I am impressed.*"

"Why?"

"*It is a good question.*"

"Let's chalk it up to my temporary sobriety."

"*Very well then. Had I been presented with a thing such as myself in the brief moments of my mortal being, I would have described myself an omen, a threat to my spiritual existence.*"

Josie laughed. "I'd agree."

Skelly nodded.

"*We have had many names, and you know them all—angel, Valkyrie, ghost, demon, god, witch, siren. Each of those carries only a whisper of our true being.*"

Skelly leaned in as if to whisper, a feat of which she was wholly incapable.

"*We are not beings at all, Little Bird. No being could do us justice. We are much more basic than that.*"

Josie snorted despite herself. "What could be more basic than a god?"

"*Tell me, what do you feel when you think me god or an angel or a demon?*"

"Annoyed."

"*Curious. Indulge me.*"

Josie felt unstable. She wasn't sure if her wariness was due to this metaphysical line of questioning or the torn-up earth of her yard or Skelly's sudden twist of tolerance for Josie's stupidity, but with every breath, she was more certain she was approaching an unignorable signpost.

"I've never subscribed to gods, and I do not incline to start now. Sometimes I feel like God is nothing more than a license for humans to behave monstrously in the name of the unnamable. A convenient out for our most primal flaws."

"*Primal flaws, you say. What then would you call a woman screaming into what she assumes is a void, only to discover she's been screaming into the faces of those very unnamed? Is that the fault of a god? Or her own? Are you somehow more responsible because you refuse the name god?*"

"Are you talking about me? Because I think you have me confused with someone else, Skelly. I've never much screamed about anything."

"*We may not always be aware of the energy we force upon the world, but that doesn't release us of our responsibility to it.*"

"Tell me when I've screamed then!" she screamed.

"*Perhaps it is best if you tell me.*"

With that, the ground began to shake again. Skelly dipped her chin, gazing at her feet as if just as taken aback by the act of rebellion as Josie was.

"*It seems I have other matters to attend to, Little Bird. Think on it tonight, for I fear tomorrow is a new day, whether we are ready for it or not.*"

"And if I'm not ready?"

Skelly shrugged.

"*Then you'll have chosen which side you prefer, and I'll no longer be able to help you.*"

STILL DAY EIGHT

THE TREMORS WERE slight at first—so much so that Josie chalked the first few up to her own unsteadiness. It wasn't until a commotion began to bristle in the cul-de-sac that she realized they weren't completely contained within her living room. Her neighbors congregated in the center of the street, gesticulating as they rattled anxiously to one another in unison. They were far enough away that Josie couldn't hear their words, but close enough that she could understand what they meant. The woman with the school-aged kids kept turning her head back to her own house, occasionally shooing one of her curious offspring back inside. Matt or Mike or whatever his name was kept fidgeting with the terry cloth towel stuffed in his back pocket—removing it to wipe the sweat from his brow every few minutes despite the mild weather. There were a few more she didn't recognize, each with protective postures that released on occasion to emote the unusual nature of the evening.

She wasn't sure how long she'd been staring at them through the window, but by the time a particularly strong quake shook her from her reverie, the clock blinked four o'clock. The power had gone out at some point, though she wasn't sure when. Her neighbors, however, didn't budge from their collective wreath of community. It appeared only Sue and Josie were absent, a topic not lost on the group, who pointed in her direction as if cognizant that she'd been watching them from the shadows for however long.

What would they say if she told them the truth? If she marched into the center of their little group and said, "Folks, have I got something that will blow your damn minds." She could direct them to her ravaged property and introduce them directly to the creator of their discomfort. And Skelly, if she appeared at all, would wave at them. She'd introduce herself, ever congenial as they fled. Boy, what would they think of that?

The earth shook again, this time with an unignorable ferocity. The curtain slipped from her fingers as she steadied herself. Po launched at the curtain as if to punish its disobedience.

Josie patted his head as he barked. "It's okay, little guy. Just a little shake."

This latest tremor drew a new set of shrieks from the cul-de-sac, and Josie was struck with an intense need to watch her neighbors. Perhaps she should have said something as shingles shattered to the concrete outside her house—*get your kids, get everyone else, you're safest in the middle of the street than stuck inside the house*—but she didn't. As far as she knew, most of the neighbors were cordial with one another, but she never saw the tell-tale signs of good neighborship. No plastic-wrapped bundles of hot cocoa left on doorsteps during the holidays, no "Hey, Bob" or "Hey, Janet" as they passed one another on evening walks. Nothing to stand out besides the soft nod of acknowledgment whenever accidental eyes met. This distance was one of the reasons Josie liked it here—it was predictable. Calm and safe.

But that calm was no longer. The sequestered children sprung from their house, toward their mother who wrapped the three of them against her stomach, as the others gripped the shoulders and shirts of the person nearest to them. They looked like a flock of ducklings, shivering and scared and searching for relief. Josie was almost compelled to put them at ease.

Don't worry, folks, I got this handled. Nothing to lose teeth over, just got myself a pesky skeleton problem. You know what I'm talking about, right?

Of course, she did not have things handled, and she had little idea what Skelly was preparing to spill onto the world, but somehow things seemed simpler when isolated to her little yard.

Josie might have been content to watch them all night had it not been for Sue. She'd announced herself to the group with the creak of her front door. She sauntered toward the group, unconcern apparent by the jovial swagger of her hips. A few of the grim expressions broke upon her approach, born into sincere smiles at the sight of her. These were grins of familiarity, of comfort, and Josie was immediately panged with surprising emotion, understanding at once that she had not been the only neighbor Sue had taken an interest in.

Because, of course, she wasn't. Sue was blunt and pragmatic, but social all the same. It was easy for Josie to mistake a person's interest in her as a likeness of spirit, not many had the fortitude to break down her stiffness, but it was exactly the type of person like Sue to succeed. A person like Josie wouldn't bother to even learn her name.

This was how she'd always been, even as a kid. Her summers were spent inside drawing, reading, and playing video games. She'd swim in the stock tank, pretending to be a mermaid like every other girl her age that'd seen the Disney movie. Dad would mow the lawn or bury himself in his work shed building remote control boats that he'd drive across the stock tank as she splashed, trying to sink them. Sometimes, Mom would drink tea and watch from the kitchen, sometimes smiling, sometimes an unreadable expression tackling her face from all corners. Josie had always taken it as disdain, but she'd seen it too many times on her own face to know the real meaning. If not for the curtain, she was certain she'd see that same expression reflected from the window.

That's just how things had always been—Josie and Dad against the world, which Ma was always quick to point out.

"You two will miss me when I'm gone," she'd say. "Who else will fold your underwear?"

Josie took this as a challenge, often stirring up her sock and underwear drawer the moment new clothes were placed inside. The act infuriated her mother, and to that Josie would claim her triumph, running into the grip of her dad. "I don't need anyone to fold my underwear. Take that, Mom!"

As she aged, the innocent jabs evolved into a steep rift between the family. Ma had always wanted more children, but Dad didn't. They argued over it in their mocking way on so many occasions that it became a running gag.

Oh, isn't that a cute baby? Don't you know how cute another one of ours would be?

Cute as a heart attack, Dad would say, winking at her if Josie was within earshot.

In the end, Dad won out. And while he and Josie made their mark together, father and daughter, sailing the seas and poking fun at a world in which neither of them felt they belonged, Ma floated along their peripherals, watching everything happen without her.

Then Dad got sick. Even though years had passed, the words stuck like hatpins in her throat. Theory went that time would ease the pain, or at least the sting would dull and become less frequent. But that hadn't been the case. Every morning and every night Josie had to actively keep the dread of illness, still pungent as ever, from cornering her into a crisis. She felt stupid, trapped as if she was doing something wrong. Not processing the loss properly. The divorce certainly didn't help, because that's exactly the words Stuart used in his letter. *You need help. I can't sit here anymore and watch you destroy yourself.*

She burned that letter, not entirely sure if Dad's death wasn't a convenient out of an already failing marriage. Josie wasn't surprised, perhaps the timing, but not the breakup itself. The problem was when she went to tell someone about it. She was halfway through a text before she realized the recipient was gone and had been for months. Not that she forgot, but instinct carried her fingers to their normal place of comfort.

She couldn't bring herself to delete the message, so sent it anyway.

Well Stuart left

This was normally when her dad would respond with some stupid misspelling that she'd have to decipher.

PERHAOS ITS FOR THE BEAT
*PERHAPS
*BEST

Josie would know what he meant, but the rapid-fire responses were comforting. No one texted like Dad. Always a spurt of furious messaging with category five grammatical errors that always made her laugh. He was never quick to pick up a keyboard, at work or at home, more a sculptor than a philosopher. He wanted to be the one out in the mud and muck, fashioning a living with the skill of his hands. Josie was always the wordier of the two, which wasn't saying much for either of them. The mechanical *ping* of a new message became their own little language—a glut of them in a row usually meant a lighthearted message, something rambling and long that he felt compelled to get right. A one-noter was more somber, perhaps a reminder for the dinner plans they had later in the week. By the time she saw these, Dad had already moved on to another task, even if the phone was in her hand as it arrived. They'd grown accustomed to what required a reply, and what was better left unsaid.

That message, the one where Stuart left, required a reply that would never come. It struck her how desperately she needed it. She felt like a small girl again, peeking from the front window in anticipation of Dad's arrival from work. But she wasn't a little girl. She was a woman now, and as such should be able to handle the catastrophe of divorce like a woman should. No should's and supposed to's, just action.

So, she sent the text because she couldn't bear to delete it, as if that, not the death and cremation, was the final authority on his passing.

The next morning, she adopted Po. To this day, he was all she had.

Sue planted herself dead center of the group of neighbors, steady as they orbited her. One of the kids ran to her side, high-fiving her over something she'd said. The mom yanked him back, close to her legs. Josie could see her white-knuckle grip on his shoulder from her living room. She let the curtain drop again, sinking into the growing shadows of her home. All the lights were off, and if not for the fact that she kept shushing an agitated Po, no one would even think she was home.

She wasn't sure how long she sat there, catatonic with thought, but the day had grown dark. Exceptionally dark. The walls rattled as the tremors increased in intensity. Shouts and knocks and clatter sprung from every direction as the neighborhood jolted into panic, chaos, and uncertainty wrenching them from their homes. Someone might have knocked on her door, she wasn't sure, through all the noise. As far as anyone else was concerned, she wasn't home. She'd rather be here anyway, processing her life's choices in the dark, than swimming upstream with a bunch of terrified, strange salmon. What would she say, anyway?

Nothing. There was nothing to say to any of them.

The sun set and it was just her and Po squinting into the dark, fully aware of all the terrifying creatures that could be lurking. And while she was terrified, another more pressing sensation clawed at her chest like a rat trapped within her ribcage. She was breathing fast—so much so that blots of neon swarmed her vision. Hyperventilating was the term, but she wouldn't identify that until later.

The trembling became more frequent, more violent. It started in her gut, a rumbling like indigestion, and buoyed out of her until the glassware in her kitchen clinked together. Perhaps she was crazy, but the shaking seemed to be localized in her house—not around it or underneath, but inside. Inside her. Probably projecting again.

She closed her eyes. The tremors drew from her center and blossomed in all directions, and as it did, the vibrations pinged off something else, like wreckage in a vast ocean. Not entirely sure how she could know, she felt certain she wasn't alone, that there were others out there channeling *something*, and just as she was nearer to figuring out exactly what they were, the shaking would pique and jar her back into her living room.

She realized after some time that she hadn't fed Po, hadn't heard from the little guy at all. Her lap was conspicuously empty, as was the rest of the couch. The house was blanketed in black, and she couldn't see much farther than five feet in front of her, but she didn't see him in that space either.

"Po?" Catching herself against the wall, she listened for the jingle of his collar.

"You want a treat?"

Silence.

That was the magic word, the combination of letters that sent tiny puppy feet at a furious scrape against the floor. Treat was her ultimate play in getting Po to do anything. The fact that he hadn't come screaming through the house at its name caused her insides to collapse.

Darting through the house, she tried flipping on the lights, but none of them worked. Po didn't respond to any of her calls, and her mind soared with terrible thoughts of his demise—he'd escaped the house and gotten lost, he'd choked and died as she was stewing in the other room oblivious to his suffering, he'd been dognapped, hit by a car, fallen into the pit in her backyard.

The dread of realizing he wasn't inside the house and remembering the massive hole caused by Skelly's rage slammed into her all at once. A choking feeling, one she hadn't experienced in years, crept like fast-moving bile up her throat, exploding in a noise akin to a gurgle.

The yard was far away, farther than she remembered, the doorknob slipped in her sweaty hand, but she made it outside. Out here was just as bleak as inside—there were no streetlights, no buzzing of everyday evening life, occasionally a car honked in the distance and sirens still rang like sad, cavernous echoes. She immediately spotted Skelly, now returned and gazing at her, stroking a conspicuous tawny lump laying across her boney lap.

"Po?"

The dog lifted his head, ears back, and whined.

"What did you do to him?"

"*I didn't do anything to him, he just jumped in my lap.*"

Skelly ran her knuckles over the top of Po's head, catching the small groove in between his eyes just like Josie would. She might have charged at her, but there was no way to cross. The vines were wild, whipping behind Skelly like the discordant tentacles of a sea monster breaching the surface.

"Give me my dog."

"*Call him. We won't let him fall.*"

"I did call him. He's too scared to cross the gap."

"*How do you think he got over here?*"

"Your vines."

"*My vines?*"

There was a heavy emphasis on "my" that Josie didn't like. "Yes, *your* vines. You snatched him up. Now you're holding him hostage until I give you whatever the hell it is you want."

"I would have thought you understood more about how I operate by now, Little Bird."

"Get your fucking hands off Po!" Rage, unhinged and full of sparks, ignited in her chest. She was shaking—her skin vibrating from the heat of her rage. Had she the ability, she'd have thrown herself at Skelly and ripped her to pieces. She'd have crushed her leering, empty skull under her heel. She'd have set the house on fire just to make sure any surviving piece of the wretched skeleton burned to a cinder.

But she couldn't. She was just another version of her own, stupid castrated self. Her only lifeline, her precious baby pup, was trapped just ten feet out of reach and she couldn't help him. She was a tantruming toddler, and nothing more.

"Have you ever considered he came here for comfort?"

"Comfort from what?"

"From you."

"Oh, that's rich. As if you haven't fucked with my head enough, now you want to set me at odds with my dog?"

"I'm only asking if you've considered it."

"I think it is evident that I have not."

"Then you should. He is terrified."

"Because of you."

"Funny, how little he thought of me until now."

That was quite the fuck enough of that. "Come on, Po. Let's go inside."

Po tilted his head to her but did not budge from Skelly's lap.

"Come on, buddy. Come on. I'll give you a treat."

Skelly peeled her hands away from the dog, placing them serenely on the armrests of her throne. Then, she tilted her head toward Josie, an indication that she wasn't stopping Po from going anywhere. Still, the little dog refused to leave her side.

Desperation clung to Josie's calls, each more pitched and panicked than the last. "Make a path for him, at least. Come on, Po! It's safe. I promise."

Vines scabbed over the gap, tight enough to prevent even the daintiest paw from slipping through. "Po! Come!"

She tried to calm herself, but the ends of herself unwound with every ignored command.

"*He doesn't understand you.*"

"Like hell, he doesn't."

"*Oh, he knows what you're saying, just not who you are.*"

"What kind of garbage is that? Of course, he knows who I am! He's not stupid."

"*If only you felt how he trembles.*"

"The entire world is shaking, everything is shaking ..."

"*So you feel it, Little Bird? Do you finally feel it? A perfectly still world, and then an unsettledness. Like an ache in your chest, a leaden dread that drags your innards through the eyehole of a needle. You feel it, don't you?*"

"I ... don't understand."

"*Yes, you do. Po is afraid of you, the earth is rebelling, and you feel like shit. What I find annoying is that you require such longwinded explanations of your own condition.*"

Skelly might have continued to speak, but Josie was already about six progressions deep into a professional level blackout. She was staring at Po, his beady eyes glazed over under the ever-bright moon. His face was all she saw—an endless reflection of his retreat from her. Everyone's retreat—a terrible white, a bed, lights both too dim and too abrasive. A diagnosis and the way an empty wine bottle clunks on the tile, sometimes shattering. A door and a door and a door, all of them full of cobwebs, swinging on desperate broken hinges. So many doors and windows and people just on the other side, each of them screaming and screaming and none of them ever hearing the other. Screaming all alone. Into the void. Screaming at everyone else while they screamed in turn.

The exact moment of completion to her mental collapse occurred somewhere between shutting doors and screaming, punctuated by a wretched, foreign noise pooling inside her head. Skelly was screaming at her, just screaming. Or someone was.

Josie couldn't discern the loose hang of her bottom jaw, the gasping of her lungs as they emptied into the night. She was completely oblivious to the fact that it was she who screamed.

"*Oh, Little Bird. My Little Bird. I am so sorry.*"

Sorry? Sorry for what? Sorry for existing? Sorry for coming here? She wanted Po, her friend, her only friend. She wanted her fucking dog and then she wanted to run away so none of this bullshit could follow her. But Po shrunk from her. She lunged across the vines toward him and he cowered as she neared.

Skelly was many things, but she wasn't a liar, and she wasn't lying now. Po was terrified of her.

"You too?" she said repeatedly.

Her skin felt like cockroaches—squirming and desperate to be free of her. She rambled now, words she'd kept tucked inside the deepest folds of her heart flowing on the current of her disassociation.

Then, a familiar voice. One she'd associated with disdain and ambivalence for days. A voice so loathsome she'd gladly gouge her eyeballs from her head with a screwdriver to be free of it. Still, the voice was the only sound with the integrity to slice apart her high-level panic attack. It was the only sound she could understand now.

"*Little Bird … I think it is finally time for you to tell me your story.*"

She swayed on her feet, dropping to her knees against a

rush of vines. They caught her, dampening the blow, and gently laid her against their strength. "What should I tell, Skelly? What on earth could I possibly tell you?"

Skelly responded with measured hesitance. "*Everything.*"

"Everything? There isn't an everything. Nothing to suggest I've lived at all. And whose fault is it? No one's but mine. I've pissed it away, holed myself up, scared away anyone daring enough to love me. They've all left, Skelly, by design or desire, they've all left. Everyone but you."

Tears slipped free of her cheeks, dropping onto her hands.

"Stuart left. I don't blame him. I was unbearable to him. I thought ... I thought he might see me running away and chase after me. I *was* running. I didn't want what he wanted. I didn't want to live in a house with a picket fence and a bunch of fucking kids. I still don't. And I think he would have been okay with that if I'd told him. But I didn't. I went on my walks and I daydreamed of being alone until I got it. Solitude smacks you, it's sharp and painful and not anything like you expected. The worst part is that I know how much he loved me. Even when he left, he loved me. I hated him. I hate him. I'm angry and hurt and I hate him for leaving. Dad had just left. My dad ..."

She couldn't bring herself to say it. Even now, even with the ground shimmering under her hurt.

"*Your dad is dead.*"

The statement landed hard. Dead. She'd avoided speaking the word aloud at every opportunity, teaching herself every other creative way to intone the meaning without that specific arrangement of letters. Gone, sick, left, resting, sleeping. Her dad had accomplished many a feat since his passing, such as closing his eyes forever, traveling to new dimensions, seeing the world from a cloud, and cultivating a garden lush with well-fed worms. He never was a man of many luxuries, and she liked the idea that he was using his new, unconstrained time to see the things he might have wanted to see.

He was a lot like her, or she was a lot like him. Maybe they were just like each other. Little bubbles weren't so bad when she could glance over at her dad's adjoining sphere, each close enough to sense but never enough to touch. Their well-manicured nearness was enough. Stuart had said she and her dad had an odd relationship. At that time, she assumed he was just taking shots at her out of anger, but maybe there was some truth to it. Maybe they weren't normal.

But was that quite so bad?

"I miss him," she said. "I miss him like I'd miss my own lungs. I don't think I've taken a true breath since he died."

Gently shifting Po from her lap, Skelly inclined her chin toward Josie.

"No, I suspect you haven't."

"And then there was Stuart. I know he had to go, he had to, we just weren't going to make it. I was … I don't know, resistant. For everything he wanted I had ten reasons that I didn't. He told me I treated him like a pet, like I just wanted him around for the sheer fact of not being alone, that it didn't matter if the person in the room was him or the bag boy at the grocery store—whose name is Kevin by the way, I would always say that because at least I knew what his name was."

"And that was important?"

"Of course not. It was a great diversion to a conversation I knew wasn't going to end well. He told me more than once, usually when he was really pissed off, that I should just go and live with my dad. And let me tell you, I was fucking tempted. How masterful of him, in the end, to leave me only once my dad was dead."

Josie sunk into the vines that cradled her. Po kept a wary distance from Josie, studying her from between a pair of shin bones.

"My mom took off to the boat, a place she never even liked and I'm sure still doesn't. She's got it all rigged up like some sort of grand testament to his memory because he loved his boat. We loved it. The boat and the water was *our* thing. Then she just invades it, begging me to come up with her and show her how everything works. She says shit like 'Let's go out like you and Dad used to,' and 'It'll be good for you,' and she's completely oblivious to how offensive I find it. As if she and I can recreate anything like that. She hates the water, gets seasick even on the dock, but she wants me to drive her all around the bay like some sort of Skipper and Gilligan bullshit, and I don't know what the fuck to tell her. How do you tell your mother that she's ruining a nice memory? That she isn't welcome and that I didn't learn to drive the boat to cart her ass around? That it was supposed to be for Dad, but he died too soon, and I never got the chance? She's grieving, too, maybe more than me. Not only did she lose her husband, but she lost me, too. I don't even return all her texts. She had to stalk me through my business to even get a sense of what I was up to. And what I was mainly up to was sulking and drinking and being angry at everyone."

Skelly reclined in her throne, shoulders stern with a sense of finality Josie could feel but not articulate.

"You do not like the dark, do you Little Bird?"

It was quite the opposite, and she was about to say so when it dawned on her that this was not the type of dark Skelly was talking about.

"You think yourself quite a patron of it, but in reality, you loathe darkness. The shadows do not suit you any more than they suit me. Many can, and do, thrive in such gloom, but you and I are not it. Shadows suffocate us, smothers us until we are nothing more than a gasp in a big wide world that cares little for such paltry releases of carbon dioxide. Or in my case, nothing at all. You and I, we

desperately need the sun. Live too long without it, and, well, you see."

Skelly pointed toward herself, plumes of dust rising from their settled places as she swiped at the air.

"What about Sue?" she asked.

"What about her?"

"You found her first, didn't you?"

"Did she tell you what I asked of her?"

"No."

"She is not the first. She is one of an incalculable many. I've been at this for a long time, Little Bird, and I'm tired. I'm afraid my particular brand of existence is no longer conducive to our desired end goal."

"Whose end goal?"

"You think I'm the only one of me?"

"How am I supposed to know?" She really needed a drink. Now more than ever. She was sticky and sweaty with need. Head pounding with need. Fingers trembling with need.

"That word incalculable comes to mind again, both before me and after me. We are a multitude. We are constant. We are trans-dimensional beings, imbued with the souls of history. We are enforcers. We are compassion."

The vines slithered around her body as she spoke. Josie's ass hit the dirt as vines strapped themselves to Skelly's form. For the first time, she saw Skelly as she might have been—vines roped themselves into delicate tendons, fleshed into taut muscles, lurched from her back into squirming, winglike shapes. A spear of thorns materialized in her palm, her grip visibly tightening around its shape. She thrust it into the sky, her face eyeless and smooth save for a mouth, working her jaw into words that no longer reverberated from the invaded space inside Josie's head, but from Skelly's own, fully formed chest. Her body writhed with a Medusa-like intensity.

"And we are here to stay."

And just like that, the vines snapped away in an instant. Skelly was back to being Skelly, while Josie rubbed her butt cheeks in awe. Skelly was both magnificent and terrifying.

"For a while, at least. A year, minimum."

Josie stood, a churn in her gut threatening to take her down again. She really, really needed a drink. "What are you here to do?"

Skelly paused, whether for effect or thought, Josie wasn't sure, but when she spoke again her booming voice was ominously soft.

"Would you like to hear a story?"

Josie faltered to respond. She both did and did not want to hear this story. Her knees struggled to keep her upright beneath the strain of withdrawal and the ground's vicious trembling.

She wanted to say yes, but what came out was, "I need a drink."

The split in the yard shook, dust billowing from its maw like smoke. From within it, she could see movement—slithering.

"I hate that I need a drink, but I need a fucking drink. I need one immediately."

"Do you mind if I join you?"

"For what? A drink?"

"It's been a considerable amount of time since my last."

"I wish I could say the same."

"We are fragile creatures, Little Bird. Easy to break."

Vines snapped to attention as she rose from her seat, plummeting themselves in between the two of them, threading together to form a low, flat table. Skelly ambled forward until her shins touched, then sat on the ground. The two were eye to eye before Josie spoke.

"Ice?"

"Neat, if you please."

"A poor choice for the cheap vodka I'm serving."

"Let me worry about that."

Still lingering at the base of the now empty throne, Po made a light yelp as Josie turned her back to head for the house. The gap between writhed and she paused at the edge of it, remembering what Skelly had said—*we won't let him fall.*

So, she cast a foot into the abyss, hoping and praying the same protection extended to her as well. If anything, Skelly was a pragmatic soul and wouldn't allow all this work—whatever it was for—go to waste over a dog. Then again, pragmatic as she was, Josie could hear the conversation in her head as Skelly explained to Sue what had happened to her. "*I thought she was going to fetch the drinks, instead she lunged into an endless pit. Shame, really.*"

Skelly was as multifaceted as a spider's eye, and before Josie had even processed all the possibilities of her demise, she found herself inside her own kitchen, Po yipping in her arms. She'd been so preoccupied by imagining Skelly's twisted rationalism that she'd auto-piloted herself toward Po and back in front of her refrigerator without thinking.

"Seems to be when I do my best work, isn't it?" she said, and after throwing the pup a well-earned milk bone, she snatched up a pair of mismatched whiskey glasses, filling each as high as the rim with crappy vodka.

Bottle tucked under her arm; the glasses made a satisfying clink as she set them on the newly formed table.

Skelly curled her bones around the glass nearest to her, and Josie caught herself staring at the strange combination of those bones, the aged glass, and the refraction of them through the clear liquid. These pair were all that remained of both a wedding gift and an impulse purchase at Target after she and Stuart had closed on their first home together. Stuart had been annoyed that she'd spent money on a new set of glasses when they already owned a set.

"We need to properly celebrate, and the nice ones are still packed," she had probably said.

"What are you really celebrating, though? The house or the booze?"

"Why not both?"

They would have clinked glasses, smiling at his little jab. Sure, she had a penchant for a snifter of brandy—or whiskey or beer or gin or—after a long day, but they were young and in love and had the rest of their lives to sober up and settle down. Those glasses had been for right then, that moment, something special for them to look back on from their retirement villa and reminisce.

How swiftly the newlywed delirium had dissolved, how crushing the blow of actual partnership. How deeply she needed those drinks—the very thing she craved for relief becoming the vehicle to her end, the last memory of the glassware being the fleshless grip of death.

"It's warm," she said as if that was important. Not much was worse than lukewarm vodka.

"*It is sufficient.*"

"How will you drink it?"

"*The same way I always have.*"

Skelly tossed her skull back, hurling the booze into the empty space between her spine and ribcage, liquid splashing against her bones with gusto.

Josie did the same, emptying the rest of the bottle equally into their glasses.

"Can you taste it?"

"*Not in a literal sense, but I have many memories of alcohol. Something about the act of it conjures up all sorts of ... feelings. There are memories in it.*"

"Memories of your former life?"

"*When you live as long as I have, Little Bird, your memories become jumbled. It is difficult to decipher which of these experiences still belong to me.*"

Josie sipped her drink, struck with the idea that she ought to savor the taste. "That sounds ... I don't know. Sad."

"*Really? I've never thought so.*"

"I suppose it's not terrible to forget some things."

Skelly doused herself in her second drink, missing her throat entirely. There was something deranged in seeing the wet stain her bones, chaotic chance spilling over her teeth and dripping onto the ground at her feet. Josie smoothed a shudder creeping over her skin, hoping Skelly wouldn't notice.

"*Only one image persists. I cannot shake it, despite my best efforts. It haunts me through the millennia, through eternity, a defiant pulse radiating throughout my corpse.*"

"I should have reminded you," she said. "Booze has a way of drudging up old aches like no other earthly concoction known to man."

"*I remembered. I drank it anyway.*"

For once in her small, petty life, Josie sensed, and obeyed, the indication that she should stay quiet.

"*Feet, of all things. I still see feet.*"

"Haunting feet?"

"*Little feet. Toes and heels and unwrinkled skin.*"

Josie nodded. "A child's feet."

Skelly said nothing.

"And you've carried this image with you all this time? These ominous feet?"

"*You might wonder how you could possibly forget such things, but you do. You forget everything that mattered to you once because there is so much noise. The thing is that I never grieved the loss. I welcomed it. I have taken solace in my distant, forgotten memories. Back in the past, they don't feel like much worth remembering. Sometimes that is a gift. Yet, no gift can last forever.*"

"Are you dying? Is this what everything has been about?"

"I am not dying, but I am no longer needed. We need others. We need those that belong to this world. That know it. That can actually help."

"You make it seem like wisdom is a bad quality to have."

"Everything in moderation, Little Bird. Live long enough and you'll understand how helpless one can be once they've seen everything too many times."

Skelly's words landed in a plume of displaced dust onto Josie's head as she understood at once—*for* once—exactly what was happening.

"You're searching for recruits."

Skelly indicated as much with the slight dip of her pointed index finger.

Josie couldn't contain her sudden burst of laughter. Oh boy, was this rich. Ludicrousness of the highest order. Skelly wanted recruits, wanted Josie in particular. *Her.* Desperation simply wasn't an efficient word anymore.

"Have you been cursed in some way? Landing on my doorstep of all places. Wow."

Skelly placed a hand over Josie's, covering her skin with aged bones. Vines lurched from beneath the table, twining themselves between their hands. The vines were warm and delicately tangled around her fingers so that she might not have noticed them if she'd not been staring right at them.

"Would you like to see, Little Bird? I will show you now."

She was drunk. A drunk. Vodka churned in her gut, screamed in her head. Her hands felt like they were floating away, or was that the vines? She nodded. How long had she been nodding?

And then the two of them were gone.

A disorienting sense of movement turned her stomach, but her vision was dark, and she couldn't quite make out where they were. Her body was missing, or maybe not missing, but rather displaced. A strong beat thrummed in her chest—her heart—

then fanned out. Everything was dark and black, but she still felt all the little bits of her scurry away, planting themselves. Roots. Her entire nervous system spun outside her body and was suddenly everywhere. She was everywhere.

And she saw everything.

This network, whatever it was, was immense. Not knowing what to do, a familiar voice chimed in with simple instructions.

"Say hello to our sisters."

Josie didn't know what to say, not that she could speak anyway. There were others, so many others. She knew them instantly, felt them as her heart twined around theirs. They were the vines. The vines connected them. What they saw, she saw. What she felt, they felt. A mere hitch of her breath sent a shiver throughout a millennia's worth of these sisters. Though many had since lost their corporeal form, they were still present and alive. Their lives flickered before her, their deaths and knowledge, too. The pressure was exhausting. She was fit to burst.

The world had no idea just what was knocking at their feet. The Earth couldn't hold them much longer. It shivered and shook as they pressed their way out. Some were already topside, those like Skelly and a hundred or so others all over the world. The rest were biding their time, awaiting ... something. A call to arms.

Just as the pressure became too much, just as she felt ready to explode, her world snapped back into existence.

Josie was back in her yard, Skelly cross-legged on the ground in front of her. Vines ravenously circled them.

Sweat poured over her and she trembled so viciously Skelly had to grip her by the shoulders to steady her. "What was that? Who were they?"

"They are what is coming. They are my sisters. They are your sisters too now, no matter what you choose."

"What are they waiting for?"

"*Me.*"

"What are you, their queen? Jesus, I need a drink. Where is the vodka, Skelly? Where did you put it?" Josie asked, panicked.

"*No such thing as a queen among us. It is simply a matter of consent. We must all agree before we act, and my only condition was that they wait until I find a suitable replacement or decide that one does not currently exist. But they are getting tired of my antics. They won't wait much longer.*"

"What have you all agreed upon then?" She was sure she was going to throw up, which was the least of her current concerns.

Releasing her, Skelly rose to a stand, bones creaking under the strain. Had they always done so and she just never noticed?

"*We have agreed to protect you, despite how aggressively you may rebuke us. Life is precious, Little Bird, and so infinitesimally rare that it must be guarded at all costs, no matter how stupidly some of the living behave.*"

Josie felt something on her chest—her own finger, as she pressed it hard to her skin with dismay. "And you want me to … be involved?"

"*Like I said, I'm desperate.*"

She'd never understood the idea of an out-of-body experience until now. Time stopped existing. Her world and everything she thought she knew turned over on itself, and she was sitting there in the wreckage being asked to live forever. Part of her watched from a safe distance somewhere overhead, voice just out of earshot. If she strained enough, she might have heard the words, "Get the fuck out of there!" But she didn't strain, and she didn't hear them.

Po is what brought her back into herself. Consumed by total hysteria, he had launched himself at the backdoor, his football body slamming uselessly against the glass. Her line of sight was blocked by creeping vines, she and Skelly enveloped by the growing cyclone of plants that spun around them. She glared at the skeleton for an answer to an unanswerable question.

"Po is scared," she said.

"*Dogs are smart.*"

"What would happen to him?"

"*He would live out his life, then he would die. They will all die, eventually. Everyone you know. Everything you love. They will die and you will not.*"

"What sort of existence is that? To watch everyone I love die? And to keep going as if they never mattered?"

"*Oh, they matter, Little Bird. They are what matters most. To deny oneself the sweet release of death is the ultimate sacrifice. Few are willing to make it. I would understand if you choose to decline.*"

"Sue declined."

"*Yes, as did the rest.*"

Po launched himself at the door again and again, so much so that she worried he would give himself a concussion. With a raise of her hand, Skelly parted the vines down the middle.

"*Go to him.*"

Frozen in place for a moment, Josie's sense returned and she sprinted toward her dog. Po wailed the moment he spotted her, paws to the glass. As she flung the door open, he jumped into her arms, trembling so fiercely she thought he was convulsing.

Here, on the cold floor of her kitchen, she completely and utterly lost her shit. Layer by layer, she unraveled while cradling her beloved pet. His nails scratched red grooves into her skin as he clamored over her, refusing to leave her but also refusing to sit still.

"It's okay," she said, fully aware that this situation was not. "It's okay, I promise. You'll be okay, buddy. I'll make sure of it. You will always be okay."

His puppy eyes watered. He was panting as if he'd been parched for days. His tiny heart pounded like a hummingbird.

She was drunk and emotional and terrified and also drunk. Her feet were sloppy and her balance off-kilter as she carried Po to the couch. She needed to sit down and think. She needed to really *think* about what was happening. She needed Po to calm down and be okay. She needed help.

"I don't know what to do, Po. I don't know what to do at all."

The ground shook again, a deep rumble that originated miles below, somewhere deep and dark. The sisters. The Sirens—or at least that's the name Josie chose to describe them. She heard a sound in the kitchen like loose change hitting the floor—Dad's helmet bank.

They will die and you will not.

And what of it? They already die while she does not. Or they leave. But as Po shivered in her lap, licking the salt from her fingertips, she knew she couldn't leave him. She couldn't do it. Sure, he was just a dog, but she refused to be that person.

The sky was so dark—had it always been this dark?

Turning, she flung the curtain wide, in her haste ripping the entire thing from the wall. Po yelped, startled, yet remained glued to her skin.

She was not surprised this time.

She stomped to the door, swinging it open with such force that the knob stuck into the drywall.

More vines.

Good.

Good. Let the vines stay. In fact, that was better.

Voices thrummed just on the other side, frightened, wailing things. People were crying—her neighbors. Josie wondered if Sue cried for her, too, quickly squashing the idea from her head. Sue wasn't the type. Sue didn't cry for anyone, not because she didn't feel, but because she'd gotten all her crying out ages ago. She was hardened. She'd seen all this and turned it down, handing

172

the power and wisdom of the world back into Skelly's palms and saying, "No, thank you."

And for what? To live a nomad's life, constantly coaxing broken, unstable humans out of their cycle of self-destruction? How many more of her were out there, watching over their shoulders, knowing what lies just under the pathetic thinness of our world? Could she stand to be one of them, too?

Would there be anything left to stand after this?

Po was barking wildly, the more familiar bark of intrusion. Josie saw why—there was a wriggling at her feet. Vines meandered their way inside the house, spreading virus-like over the drywall, snapping light fixtures into pieces, knocking over furniture. At once, her floor was nothing but bustling plants and shattered pieces of glass and wood. Po howled.

She tried to calm him, shushing him like she might an infant, but he was too riled for that. "It's okay, Po," she said. "I'll burn it down before they touch you."

She wasn't even sure who she meant by "they." She was probably the one he should be running from anyway.

Her home was unrecognizable—ivy-like plants ripped through the cushions of her couch, snaked onto the countertops, plates and cutlery trembled and shattered to the floor as they poked their way through every crevice of her house. And she watched. Just watched the botanical destruction, gripping Po with every ounce of her remaining strength.

Her living room was a jungle, and she extended a hand toward the closest green creeper, hesitant to touch it as if it might latch onto her and never let go. She imagined herself a captive, slapped against the wall like a host body in some alien hatchery. The thought passed with a shiver, just enough to give pause, but not enough to stop her.

A small sprout emerged as her fingers caressed the smooth

green. Yanking her hand away, she watched as it unfolded from its center, exposing a familiar white flower.

"Sue," she said, whipping around to face a sea of flowers that hadn't been there mere moments ago. Po grunted, then kicked himself out of Josie's arms. Waddling his way to the nearest bud, he sniffed it as if it might explode, then, somehow satisfied, trotted back to her feet.

Josie sat on what remained of her couch, Po leaping back into her lap. She tried to remember what her furniture used to look like—hell, it was only a minute ago that the vines arrived—but couldn't. How big was her television? Where had the pictures been? How could she forget so quickly? She should be more bothered that she couldn't put any of the pieces back together.

Instead, she laid her palm to the greenery searching them. "Can you hear me?" she asked.

"*Yes.*"

Skelly appeared at her side, arms strung casually along the back of the couch.

"*Nice place.*"

"No, it isn't."

"*It could have been.*"

"Maybe if someone else had lived here."

"*That's a given. With you, it's just sort of sad.*"

Josie shrugged. "Can I ask you another question?"

"*Sure.*"

"Why do you call me Little Bird?"

Pausing a finger to her chin, Skelly feigned consideration before answering.

"*Seemed appropriate. You're the type to stay in the nest until vigorously shoved.*"

"And you knew that before even meeting me, did you?"

"*I've known you far longer than you realize.*"

174

"That isn't a comfort."

"*It isn't meant to be.*"

"How do you choose?"

"*However I like, and the others do the same. We all have our reasons for looking where we do.*"

"Why look here then?"

"*Because you're a mess. A cynic, and a drunk. People usually end up that way because their hearts have been battered beyond recognition, which is a surefire way to be sure they have one to begin with. Besides, happy people don't need interruption. If they have mastered such an elusive quality, who am I to disturb it?*"

Josie shifted in her seat to allow Po a bit more room. "What are the others like?"

"*They're like me. Only much different.*"

"Fuck, okay." Her instinct was to argue, but by now she'd grown so accustomed to Skelly's twisted way of speaking that she understood what she meant. "They're just like people. Regular, everyday, annoying people."

Skelly placed a hand on Josie's shoulder. It was cold and surprisingly light.

"*Yes, I'm sorry to say.*"

"And what will become of you?"

"*I will rest.*"

"You mean you'll die?"

"*No such luck. It will be more like a nap that is constantly interrupted, yet that offers more peace than I have now.*"

"What of me? What am I supposed to do with this?" She ran her fingers through Po's fur, noting its silkiness, the way her hands caught on the bare patches of his balding underbelly, and his too-long nails in desperate need of a trim.

"*No one is asking you to change the world, Little Bird. Only your small part of it.*"

Josie took her time to think while she petted Po. His shivering had subsided, and his breathing had returned to its usual, agitated rhythm. Skelly gazed around the room as if never having laid eyes upon such a simple place. Her head cocked to the side more than once as her bony fingers slid across the stained fabric of the couch, vines parting in anticipation of her touch.

"This couch is old," Josie said. "Stuart didn't want it."

"*I like it very much.*"

"You do?" This amused her for some reason. Skelly, the great and powerful creature, in love with her ugly couch. "Why?"

"*This fabric is simply perplexing.*"

"It's microfiber."

Skelly placed a hand to Po's snout, which he nudged enthusiastically for pets.

"If you had the choice, would you choose this life again?"

"*A thousand times over, though only due to my ignorance at the time of making such a choice.*"

"Sounds like college."

Skelly nodded. "*I have only one regret.*"

"How fortunate."

"*Oh, no, it's just that I've forgotten the rest.*"

"What is it then? The one regret that stuck?"

"*I wish I'd have gotten the chance to wear a nice dress. I quite enjoy nice dresses.*"

"Oh, well, I might have a dress of two around here." She thought about this. "Well, I might. I can't recall wearing any dresses recently."

"*A miscalculation on your part.*"

"Perhaps." She was already out of her seat, invigorated by a sudden agenda. "I must have something."

"*Do note that I specified a nice dress.*"

Vines cleared from her path as Josie marched toward her

bedroom. The place was a disaster—blankets crumpled on the floor, books she'd always planned to read but never did, stacked and covered in dust in the corners, hamper erupting clothes like a multi-headed hydra, and more dirty socks strewn about than she was pretty sure any one person was fit to own. She'd expected the infestation of greenery to have seeped into this part of the house, but her room remained just as she remembered it.

She marveled at how easily a day mutated into eternity in her mind.

The accordion doors of her closet creaked open, and she began tearing through the paltry pieces still managing to hang from a proper hanger. The rest laid in a lump of semi-cleanliness on the floor.

"What do you think of floral prints?" she asked, and Skelly answered from the bed, now propped with one elbow atop the sheetless mattress.

"They're fine."

Josie held up an old cotton maxi dress she'd kept since high school. It didn't fit her anymore, yet it had still been packed and moved from house to house over fifteen years.

Dropping the skirt back to the floor, she said, "That's a no."

Clothes sprang from her hands as she eviscerated her collection of clothing. "How insistent are you on the dress being clean?"

"Considering where you keep the bulk of your clothes, I'd say cleanliness is not an issue."

"I have a skirt." She fanned her hand around a floor-length polyester skirt with tapered edges that reminded Josie of Morticia Adams. "I wore it to a Bat Mitzvah."

"I like it."

"But it's not a dress. You said dress."

"The skirt is sufficient."

"Sufficient is not sufficient."

"Sufficient is plenty."

"I could sew something."

"You don't know how to sew."

"I could learn." As she spoke, the ground shook and she fell on top of the discarded clothes.

"I think you overestimate how much time we have."

The bed shifted about six inches south, rattling along the tile as the earth roared. Skelly, however, hadn't budged an inch and now partially hovered in mid-air.

Josie leaned against the dark wall of her closet, annoyed. She had to have more dresses. She tried recalling certain events of her life where she'd have worn them, but even if the event came to memory, her outfit didn't. Surely, she wore a dress more than just on her wedding day.

Just as she thought it, as if materializing out of the ether, she turned to see a familiar, black dress bag. She'd overlooked the garment for two reasons—one, the closet was dark and she was frenzied, and two, she distinctly remembered throwing it in a dumpster.

In fact, she was certain she'd tossed this dress in a dumpster. This particular meltdown happened in front of Sue's old house—one of the few times the landlord had bothered fixing anything—roof repair. She'd just moved in and finally gotten around to unpacking her clothes. She was about six drinks in at the time, and when she pulled the dress bag out of the box she was overcome with a distinct, sickening feeling that might have also been the beginnings of a hangover. She stomped out front and threw it into the rented dumpster with all the discarded roof shingles and rotting lumber. The rest of the night was effectively scorched out of her memory, but the next morning she'd unsuccessfully tried to contain her sobbing when she discovered that the dumpster had already been hauled away.

And now, here it was. She'd recognize that dress bag anywhere.

"I think I have something," she said, caressing the edges as if a map to some ancient treasure.

Skelly did not indicate interest. Josie unzipped the bag. Blue lace spilled onto the floor. "What about this?"

"*What about it?*"

"Do you like this one?"

"*You seem to.*"

"It's my wedding dress. My feelings are mixed, at best."

But they weren't. She knew exactly how she felt about this dress—the baby blue lace monstrosity that made her look like an Easter Marshmallow Peep. The dress was delicate, but rough around the edges. She bought it off a Dillard's clearance rack to the absolute horror of her mother. Her dad, however, snorted his Pepsi through his nose when she showed him a picture. The dress was ridiculous, which was fitting because marriage was ridiculous, and still she wanted them both. She thought it would make her feel less alone.

Stuart cackled in a way she'd never heard him cackle when she showed him. He said he couldn't wait to show every person he knew his wife's hideous dress.

"I thought I'd thrown this in a dumpster," she said, avoiding Skelly's face.

"*I guess not.*"

"I was drunk. Maybe I jumped back in and saved it? I was blacking out a lot those days."

"*I could tell you what happened if you want.*"

"It doesn't matter."

"*You do realize what you are offering, don't you Little Bird?*"

Josie paused, the moment striking clear. Everything rocked back and forth like a ship caught in a storm. She could barely remain upright as she sat on the bed, Skelly's feet just inches away.

Po leaped onto the bed, grunting from the exertion. Earthquakes were tough on little dogs.

"Only if he can come."

"He cannot, but nothing says he can't remain your companion as he is now."

"What if he's scared of me?"

Skelly outstretched a hand to him, patting his head. He licked her, then pushed his scalp into her palm.

"I think he'll be fine."

Josie draped the dress over the bed. "Am I really so odd, Skelly?"

A loud crack whipped through the house as her foundation began to falter. Somewhere a large beam snapped in half.

"You're odd in your own way, yes. But others are equally odd in theirs."

"Then why do I feel more comfortable with you than I've ever felt with anyone else? I mean, there was my dad, of course, but now?"

She saw images of all the people that had skirted in and out of her life—her mom staring at the murky ocean water from the boat, Dad in his hospital bed, Stuart checking his watch as he waited for a date, Sue, entwined within the crowd of onlookers, not even bothering to stop and check on her.

"I think you might want to look outside."

Far beyond questioning Skelly by this point, she obediently went to the living room.

Shooing the vines away, she stopped at what she saw.

Flowers. White flowers in all directions. There were so many she couldn't see the houses just next door. Everything was utterly consumed. Considering her expectations, this was a pleasant surprise.

"What is going on?"

"Sue."

"Sue did this? Why?"

"*So the rest wouldn't be afraid.*"

"So, where are they then?"

"*They ran away.*" Shrugging, she added, "*Can't win them all.*"

A multitude of emotions swarmed her thoughts, but chief among them was a clarity she hadn't felt since the last time she and her dad were on the boat. For once, she knew exactly what she wanted to do.

"You'll want to hurry into that dress, I suspect."

"*Done.*"

Skelly posed beside her, occasionally pushing the straps of the dress back over her shoulder blades.

"Is this really your one regret?"

"*To simply wear a dress? No.*"

"Then what is it?"

Skelly sauntered toward the couch, vines parting to her presence. As soon as she sat on the couch, plants closed over her as if she were an old house marm watching her afternoon stories, a blanket draped over her legs.

"*Why don't you tell me?*"

"That's a tall order, my friend."

"*Try.*"

Josie sized her up, realizing at once how much she'd never noticed. Skelly folded her hands in her lap, patient and motionless. All this time Josie had easily anthropomorphized her expressions, prescribing her perpetually vacant stare to condescension and irritation and delight. Perhaps that's how Josie would have spoken, and perhaps that's why Skelly behaved the way she did.

But Josie had a difficult time believing Skelly's personality was nothing more than a Josie retrofit. There was a reason she chose Josie's door over many others, even if she was the end of a long line of candidates.

Skelly, like Josie, was simply looking for her people.

Unfortunately, *her* people, people like Josie, were the absolute worst types of people to like. No wonder she was so goddamn irritated all the time.

"Your hands are broken. The bones, I mean. I never noticed before, but the light shines through the hairline cracks in more than one place."

"*That is your answer?*"

"I'm getting there, okay?"

"*Please* do *take your time.*"

"It's not like I've done this before, you know." Po sniffed at a few budding vines, settling next to Skelly on the couch and barking every time the ground shook.

"*You do this for a living, Little Bird.*"

"Assess the greatest regrets of ancient beings?"

"*Read people.*"

"That's different." Po followed her with his eyes as she paced in front of the couch. "They're regular people. People in possession of muscle and skin, I might add."

"*How many of your clients' faces have you seen?*"

She'd gone out of her way to not put a face to any of them, though curiosity did get the better of her more than once. Jackie posted multiple videos to his Instagram of himself running laps in his driveway that she'd watched for hours one night— every one of them, going back two years. For some reason, she was enthralled. They were fascinating, most of all because she understood why he jogged for an audience. She hated that she understood, but she did. He was single, ran his business, was in relatively decent shape for a forty-eight-year-old man, and had nothing better to do on a Saturday morning than to run circles in front of his own house. He took careful pains to curate his public persona, which only made Josie even more curious about the type of person he was once the door shut behind him.

Because she knew firsthand the kind of wreckage from which that baffling phoenix arose—she'd been created there herself.

"*Consider me a client.*"

"I imagine you would like the Gold Package?"

"*Most assuredly.*"

Josie closed her eyes, hoping to tap into the work portions of her brain. The transition was surprisingly simple.

"There's not much to add that you haven't already said—you're old and tired and a little bit lonely. You've stated that it is time for the old guard to step down. Perhaps you are the last of the 'old guard' left. Not just because you are intolerable and disagreeable to every potential replacement, but because you are actively resisting the change. And your sisters are taking you to task."

"*Say this is true, tell me, why should I resist change?*"

"For the same reason we all do. It's scary. Frankly, it's about all I can think that would frighten a being like you anyway—no longer being able to be you. Very human of you, really."

"*I told you I was human.*"

"Used to be."

"*Used to be.*"

"And now what will you be?"

Skelly extended a hand.

"*I will be a friend.*"

Josie stared at the joints of Skelly's hands—the breaks and the dust and the age and the fragility of them. The smallest amount of pressure might scatter them to the floor, likely only clinging together now by the sheer might of Skelly's will.

"Perhaps that is your regret? Not having many friends?"

"*Perhaps.*"

Boy, could she relate. Josie accepted Skelly's hand and her senses exploded in an instant. Wrapping one arm around Po and the other around Skelly, Josie clung to the both of them as the center of her living room dropped into an increasingly expanding pit. Floor tiles vibrated, the drywall cracked, wooden supports toppled over, and soon they were falling.

They were going to die. They were going to drop through the earth and suffocate beneath the wreckage. Her stomach gave out and she vomited as whatever sucked them down and down and down increased in speed. She couldn't see and the air smelled like rain. Dirt and rock dusted the air.

They fell.

Josie was suddenly aware of movement around her—external sensors she never recognized before flicked alive and, as she fell, she felt other beings writhing around her, heading in the opposite direction. Up.

Then they stopped falling. The landing was gentler than she expected. Po had stopped yelping, delirious from the fall. His heart thudded viciously against his chest so that she could feel it from the outside. Josie waited for her adrenaline to level out before realizing she'd never experienced a pique. Her heart was level, she was calm. Her heart was ... not beating at all.

Checking for a pulse in the dark, she reached out toward where Skelly should have been.

"*Skelly, what happened?*"

Skelly did not respond. Josie felt around in the dark, finally catching the hem of her wedding dress. Skelly was not there.

"*For fuck's sake, do not tell me you left me here.*"

The movement once surrounding her had stilled, and she was acutely aware of her solitude. The only beings present were her and Po, and whatever was crawling up her back.

"*Fuck.*"

Whipping around, she thrashed her hands toward whatever touched her and caught the smooth, undeniable form of a vine.

Finding his voice, Po began to wail.

"It's okay, buddy. I'll figure this out."

Then the vine snaked around her feet, planting her to the ground. Before she could attempt to whip it away, she saw. She *saw*.

She saw everything. Through one vine she discovered the rest, each of them weaving through and around and behind one another. Plants wriggled toward the surface, and she followed them with her sight. There were mountains and beaches and concrete and the bottoms of feet, there were voices and trees and grass and oceans, there were fish and the sharp talons of birds. She watched these botanical wonders surface, felt them move and squirm, and then she heard—or felt, or a strange combination of the two senses—the vines being summoned.

Through the vines, she heard the voices. She heard the wild charges of the others. The other skeletons. The other sirens. Her sisters.

Finally, she returned to her current predicament. Her dress lay sprawled in the dirt. Knotted between the fabric was a scattering of loose bones.

A skeletal hand reached toward the bones and Josie yelped with relief.

"There you are."

But Skelly did not respond. The bones were cold and covered in dirt. The skeletal hand that dragged marks through their resting place was hers.

She was so used to Skelly's presence in her head she hadn't pieced together that the booming voice was *her* voice now, a familiar yet new voice. Josie reached for the skull, now tossed aside and empty. She stared, and she saw everything—saw Skelly as she was and what she will be. Saw the world that made her and those haunting feet. Felt an incapacitating rawness that threatened to grind her to dust if not for the single, watchful vine that slapped the skull out of her hands.

Lurching toward the other bones, the obnoxious vine weaved between them with calculating intent. Threading the small bones together, a sloppily constructed hand emerged from the pile, stopping just shy of Josie's face and resting on her shoulder before collapsing into nothing once again.

"Ah, so I'm not completely rid of you yet."

Vines spun into her new, skeletonized form, lifting her body off the ground.

"Watch out for Po."

She'd not so much as finished the sentence before vines swarmed around them, cocooning them within. A single tendril broke free, reaching out to pat Po atop the head before a monstrous growl shot them upward. Josie was thrown backward. She traced the sound, following it with her new sight as the surface opened up. White flowers shivered like a rolling wave as the surface ripped apart. Plants grabbed hold of her and slowly, methodically, lifted her.

The dark was a comfort, something she was so used to that she braced for the sting of sunlight despite not having any eyes.

Stopping short of a complete breach, vines thrust her just to the surfaces' edge, forcing her to haul herself the rest of the way up. One hand clinging to the vestiges of her former home and the other lifting Po to safety, she paused a minute to simply gaze at the sky. It shone a brilliant, dusky purple. The scene was quite pretty.

Then a head shadowed her view.

"Are you coming or not?" Sue cradled an agitated Po against her chest, a sort of indignance in the way she postured herself.

"Can I have even a moment?"

"You've had plenty of moments. How many more do you need?"

"I'll let you know."

And without bothering to use her arms or hands, Josie floated topside.

"I'm breathless with anticipation."

Josie noted the wreckage of her home, now a crater of debris and dirt. A severed water line sprayed rainbow hue into the air, pooling into the depression like a murky swamp. Sue's house had also collapsed on one side, her garden destroyed. The rest of the cul-de-sac, while flooded with Sue's delicate flowers, also existed in varying states of disrepair, from foundation damage to minor stucco cracks.

"*This looks bad.*"

"Your supreme ability to spill disaster into people's lives remains unchallenged."

"*Keep up the attitude and I'll leave it this way.*"

"No, you won't."

Po wriggled free, sprinting toward Josie at breakneck speed. Josie lowered a hand, and Po leaped into her. Any other time he would have tripped over himself and dropped onto his face, but she was able to account for his abnormally long body and poor coordination with astounding ease. Her new prescience was good for something, at least.

"*I'm afraid I don't know the first thing about construction.*" She indicated toward Sue's house, and then she remembered. "*Perhaps this will help?*"

Tapping into the botanical highway, she found what she was looking for buried a dozen or so feet from Skelly's remains.

At Sue's feet, she placed a gold bar.

"Where did you get this?"

"*Skelly.*"

"She never gave me gold."

"*You never asked for it.*"

"A missed opportunity."

"*Use it to pay a contractor to fix this mess.*"

"You seem to think we will be staying here."

Josie couldn't stop staring at Sue's destroyed garden. Cinder block and dirt and mayhem smothered it, or else lay trapped in the sinkhole of her own creation. Well, maybe the destruction wasn't just her creation, but she was a part of that hole. For once in her life, she was determined to fix something she'd broken.

"*I have an idea.*"

MANY DAYS LATER

JOSIE AND SUE sat at their familiar table in the garden, now flush with every imaginable native plant conceivable. Flowers spilled into the now vacant space that used to be Josie's house, the house of which was buried under the Earth. She didn't need it anymore, and the space was better suited for community space anyway. This was what Josie did now—maintain her plants all over the globe. The rest of her sisters had their own agendas, but this was hers. And she was good at it.

After splitting a shortbread cookie with Po, Sue washed the sweetness down with a large gulp of tea. Po trotted around the table legs, weaving in a figure eight between Josie's feet and settling atop the exposed bone of her metatarsals.

"I think he wants to go with you today," Sue said.

"*I don't blame him. I'm very interesting.*"

"You are something, but interesting isn't what I'd choose."

"*Don't act like you weren't my gateway to sirenism.*"

Sue snapped an obnoxious chunk of shortbread into her mouth. "These cookies are especially good this morning."

"*That's a dirty trick and you know it.*"

"For a person who has breakfast with me every morning, you sure go out of your way to not know me that well."

"*Sirens don't shed all their human qualities, especially not those of such value. Oh, shit, what time is it?*"

"Six. Why?"

"*Some teenage punks thought it'd be fun to smash every pumpkin in my northern garden. They've been restrained for thirty minutes now.*"

191

"Restrained?"

"Just a couple of vines around the ankles. They'll be fine. Figured I'd pop in and say hello before they left."

"Sounds innocent enough. Take Po or else he'll whine all day."

Josie leaned over to pet her ever-loyal pup.

"How about it, Po? Want to go terrorize some kids with me?"

"Don't you dare!"

"I'm not going to hurt them, Sue. Calm down. Usually, my presence alone is terrifying enough."

Sue sipped her tea, managing a spectacular grimace as she did. "Be nice."

"Am I ever otherwise?"

Sue shuffled her remaining cookies back into their holder, sealing the bag with a chip clip. "You sound more and more like her every day."

"Skelly?"

She nodded.

"Does the resemblance bother you?"

"It's a comfort, actually. I miss her."

"Bleh, she drives me fucking crazy."

"Tell her I said hello."

"I will."

Dog in hand, Josie summoned some vines and was gone. Until tomorrow.

Acknowledgements

I'd like to start by acknowledging my three biggest hype men—my two children and my mother, because of whom have sold multiple books of mine to otherwise disinterested elementary school educators and pool industry folk. My husband, too, deserves many thanks. His support and belief in me carried me in those dark days of "Yes, I'm still writing. No, I'm not published." He was there for me fifteen years ago when I started this insanity just as much as he is today, now with a couple of books on the shelf.

To my writing group—the people who have read my work, listened to my challenges, encouraged me through them, all while absorbing my incredibly stupid hot takes™ before they get to my main. Colleen, Delara, V, and Ally, I am grateful every day that we found each other. Also shout out to Karlo, who tolerates my loud and silly opinions more than any person unrelated to me should. I am so lucky to call all of you my friends.

To Audrey, who has designed artwork for both of my books—thank you. And to all my siblings, both biological and by marriage, who watch scary movies and stupid movies with me when I'd otherwise be a wreck over something (even if you didn't know it)—thank you.

Lastly, Lindy. I don't know how you manage to sleep and have a family and teach and publish and write and still have the sincerity of soul to uplift your anxious writers. I thank the universe every day that we crossed paths.

To anyone I might have failed to mention here, please know it is not for lack of appreciation, but more a lack of brain cells. Thank you!

About The Author

Tiffany is a writer of weird fiction hailing from Phoenix, Arizona. Her debut novel, A Flood of Posies, was released in February 2021. She has shorter published works with Luna Station Quarterly, The Molotov Cocktail, Shoreline of Infinity, and others. She lives with her husband, two children, and a menagerie of animals. Find her online at www.TiffanyMeuret.com